Never, in all her dealings with Matthew McKnight, would Cory have suspected admiration. Not from him.

She felt a quickening of her heart, and again she had to look away, unable to reconcile her memories and her own emotions with this new information. She had to stop this foray into unfamiliar territory. She had no defenses against this gentle onslaught. It was tempting to believe him totally, to accept his admiration, to think that maybe his comments, his glances, the sum total of what had been happening between them the past few days, might go somewhere else. But she didn't dare.

Books by Carolyne Aarsen

Love Inspired

Homecoming #24
Ever Faithful #33
A Bride at Last #51
The Cowboy's Bride #67
*A Family-Style Christmas #86
*A Mother at Heart #94
*A Family at Last #121

*Stealing Home

CAROLYNE AARSEN

comes from northern Alberta, where she was born, raised, married and is currently half finished raising her own family of four—if raising children is a job that's ever done.

Carolyne's writing skills were developed amid being a stay-at-home mother, housewife, foster mom and business partner in a farm and sawmilling business. She started her writing career with a weekly humor column, currently running in several rural Alberta newspapers. Writing for Love Inspired has given her the chance to indulge in her first love—romance writing—and remain true to her Christian convictions.

Through all her writing Carolyne wishes to portray how God works in our lives and the lives of families and communities. Her main goal is to show people's weaknesses and Christ's strengths.

A Family at Last
Carolyne Aarsen

Published by Steeple Hill Books™

STEEPLE HILL BOOKS

Steeple
Hill™

ISBN 0-373-87127-9

A FAMILY AT LAST

Copyright © 2000 by Carolyne Aarsen

Printed in U.S.A.

Can a mother forget the baby at her breast and have no compassion on the child she has borne? Though she may forget, I will not forget you! See, I have engraved you on the palms of my hands!

—*Isaiah* 49:15, 16

To Linda Ford, friend and fellow writer and supporter, as well as mother of numerous children and foster children. For all their help with the legalities of wills and holograph wills, I would like to thank Madelaine Wessel and Jean Gunns.

Chapter One

He looked familiar.

Cory paused, narrowing her eyes as the latest customer came through the restaurant doors. All she could see from this angle was a tall man whose sandy-brown hair had a tendency to wave and a light-brown suit jacket that sat easily on broad shoulders. Something about the tilt of his head, the way he carried himself…

I'm getting jumpy, she thought, trying to dismiss the feeling.

But if there was one thing Cory and her mother had learned over the past years was to trust their instincts, and Cory had a bad feeling about this man.

She continued wiping the table her most recent customers had just vacated, absently pocketing the tip, trying for a closer look at him. He had chosen a seat in one of the booths by the window hidden from Cory's view.

She tried to brush away the uneasiness as she

brought the dirty dishes back to the kitchen, but still couldn't stop one more glance over her shoulder.

On her return she grabbed the coffeepot, forced a smile, then turned, taking a deep breath as she walked toward the booth.

He sat with his arms folded on the table. As he turned, Cory swayed, clutching the coffeepot, the blood draining from her face.

Matthew McKnight.

And where Matthew was, her stepfather couldn't be too far behind.

What was Matthew doing here? How had he found them? She and her mother had been so careful.

The questions piled on top of each other, backing up in her mind.

Maybe it was just coincidence, she reassured herself. Maybe he just happened to be passing through.

Maybe she should get someone else to help him.

But there was no one else in the restaurant and as she paused, he turned.

And saw her.

Cory forced her feet to move toward him, her heart increasing its tempo with every step.

She stopped at his table and in spite of herself, couldn't help looking at him.

She met a pair of deep-green eyes beneath level brows. His hair waved away from his face, curling over the collar of his crisp white shirt. His suit jacket lay easily on his shoulders, it's impeccable cut reminding Cory of how much money the McKnights had.

As good-looking as ever, Cory thought with dismay at the unwelcome stab of appreciation that filtered through her angry fear.

"Hello, Cory Smith," Matthew said, his voice quiet. The tone of his voice told her that coincidence had not brought him here. He had expected to see her.

"I go by Cory Luciuk now," she said, her voice crisp. "Coffee?"

"Please."

"Menu?" Cory kept her eyes resolutely on the bubbles forming in the liquid in the cup.

"I'll just have a piece of apple pie."

Against her better judgment, Cory chanced another look. His gaze was compelling and forceful at the same time. How many times hadn't she faced those eyes as he walked past her out of the courtroom, victorious once again?

How many times hadn't she fought the disloyal, foolish hope that he would relent, that he would slow down and acknowledge her as a person, not as an opponent.

"How did you find me?" she asked, deciding the direct approach was the best. "Because I'm assuming you came, knowing I worked here."

Matthew finally looked away, toying with the cup as if trying to figure out what to tell her. "You're right. I did."

"Then how?"

"A little bit of luck and a lot of prayers."

Cory thought of the many prayers her mother sent up, prayers for release from her ex-husband, prayers that she and Cory could establish some kind of life apart from Zeke. Now, it looked as if Matthew's prayers had won. He looked up at her again. "When did you change your name?"

"Does it matter?" she asked, unable to keep the

frustration out of her voice. "You found us. But I'm sure you didn't do all that work just so we could discuss our name change."

"You're right." Matthew bit one corner of his lip, scratching his forehead with his index finger. "I need to talk to you in private, Cory."

"What about?"

"Your stepfather."

"Why am I not surprised?" In spite of her casually spoken words, she felt a tremor of apprehension.

"Can you meet me when you're off work?"

Cory felt cornered. Was he arranging this meeting for Zeke? Had she and her mother's caution all been for nothing? For a fleeting moment Cory imagined herself turning, running out of the restaurant, taking her mother and heading out of town in any direction that took them away from Matthew, away from Zeke.

Cory's grip tightened on the coffeepot as she forced herself to remain calm. Neither she nor her mother would run away anymore. They had stayed here long enough to develop friendships. People in this friendly town had gone out of their way to help them settle in. "How much is this meeting going to cost me?"

Matthew frowned. "What do you mean?"

"No one talks to a lawyer for free," she said, taking refuge in anger, hoping, praying it would cover her fear, her own foolish reaction to his good looks. "Why don't you tell me right now and get it over and done with?"

Matthew shook his head. "I'm sorry. I prefer to talk to you in private. Can I come to your home later on?"

A brief vision of the ancient bungalow that she and Joyce rented flitted through her head. She couldn't help but mentally compare it to Matthew's home in Riverview—a two-hour drive from Stratton. All dormers and gables and expensive jigs and jogs. Situated at the edge of the golf course, no less.

"No," she said firmly. "How about tomorrow morning, here?"

"I'd like to meet you sooner than that." He looked up at her, tucking one corner of his mouth under his teeth, the way he always did when he was contemplating something.

Cory felt the full force of his good looks, the charm he gave off as easily as the flame from a struck match. She almost took a step back—almost let her heart quiver in response.

"Is there someplace I could meet you after work today?" he continued.

He wasn't going to let her off, she thought. "There's a park we could go to. Turn east on Fifty-Seventh and you'll find it. I'll meet you there at 5:00."

"Okay. I think I know where it is. I'll be there."

"And I'll be back with your pie." Cory turned, sucked in a slow breath and strode away, fighting her fluctuating emotions. In spite of everything he had done to them, all the humiliation she had suffered because of Matthew's defense of her stepfather, one look at those deep-green eyes could still make her feel all fluttery again.

With another quick glance over her shoulder at Matthew she escaped to the washroom.

She turned the cold water on full blast, then bent over and splashed it on her face hoping to ease the heat in her cheeks, hoping to settle a heavy sense of foreboding.

As she toweled off her face, she glanced in the mirror. Thankfully the face staring back at her looked calm, self-possessed. With a long slow sigh, Cory threw the paper towel in the garbage, pulled open the washroom door, stepped outside and got Matthew his pie.

Matthew had his elbows on the table, his chin resting on his steepled fingers as she approached.

Attractive as ever, Cory thought, grudgingly admitting his appeal. It's the hair, she figured, those waves that made a woman want to rearrange them, the dimple that dented his one cheek when he smiled.

Cory never saw that dimple much. Matthew seldom smiled around her. He considered Cory to be beneath him and he considered Cory to be beneath his cousin Deirdre McKnight, Cory's high school friend.

Deirdre used to laugh at the way Matthew used to warn her about Cory. "He thinks you're some kind of juvenile delinquent bent on turning me astray," she had joked.

Cory had obediently laughed along, but the comment stuck with her. Each time she met Matthew she would remember it, wondering why it should bother her.

In fact, it could still bother her.

She set the plate on the table, unable to avoid looking at him. "Here's your pie."

"Thanks." He looked up at her, his expression still serious. "I'll see you later on, then."

Her only reply was a cool smile that belied the tension she felt.

The next twenty minutes were busy, but Cory didn't relax until she saw Matthew leave. She couldn't help but watch as he ducked into a snappy-looking sports car.

Expensive-looking sports car.

As Cory cleaned up his cup and plate, she found a generous tip. Stifling her humiliation, Cory picked it up. He obviously thought she needed the money. And, sadly, he was right.

The rest of her shift went quickly. The supper crowd descended, and Cory and her fellow waitresses picked up the pace. By the time Cory's shift was done, her feet burned and her head ached with tension. She wondered if Zeke was going to be with Matthew and prayed he wouldn't. Matthew hadn't given any indication that Zeke would be there.

"So, how did you do on tips today?" her friend Kelsey asked as Cory slipped on her jacket.

"Do you think I'm going to tell the daughter of the owner that? You'll want the restaurant's share."

"Don't tempt me, my dear," Kelsey Swain said with a sigh, flipping her own long, red hair free from her coat. "You always do pretty good on tips, you old smoothy. I think it's those deep brown eyes. Makes a guy think you're all soft and sweet instead of the cool and collected type that turns down dates with a joke."

"If you still want a ride to your parents', I suggest you keep a civil tongue in your head," Cory warned, pulling open the back door of the restaurant.

"No threats." Kelsey raised her hands in mock surrender as she walked through. "Please, no threats."

Cory unlocked the passenger door of her car, then got in her side of the station wagon.

"You know, Cory, when your catering business starts taking off, I sure hope you can buy yourself a decent vehicle,'' Kelsey said, glancing over her shoulder.

"Hey. Who's driving who?" Cory asked with a laugh as she backed out of the parking lot. "At least my vehicle runs."

"Yeah. You're doing better than me in that department. I'm getting tired of constantly fixing that lemon I drive. Now if I had a man in my life, that would be different. He could fix it."

"Oh, brother, don't start on that. As if men are going to be your salvation."

"Don't get all cynical on me, girl. I don't know what guy soured you on men, but I'm not like that."

"Few men are like Carter," Cory said, referring to Kelsey's former husband. Carter had died two and a half years ago, but Kelsey still talked about him.

"No. Most likely not," Kelsey said softly. "But I think I saw someone that could come close. He looked like a perfect man."

"That's an oxymoron."

"He came just before the supper rush," Kelsey continued, ignoring her friend. "Tall, with wavy hair. Killer smile." Kelsey sighed dramatically. "And a dimple. Right there." Kelsey poked her finger into a spot just beside her mouth.

Oh, goodness, she means Matthew, Cory thought with a jolt. "I don't know how you can remember him," Cory said, forcing herself to sound disinterested. "We must have served two-dozen guys since then."

"Oh, but not like him. He had a charm, a charisma that simply oozed out of him. And a fancy little sports car."

"Don't forget the dimple."

"C'mon. ~~He was definitely hero~~ material."

"You and your heroes," Cory said with mock anger. "There's no such thing. A guy is a guy is a guy."

"Speaks the cynical beauty," Kelsey teased. "Don't tell me you haven't wished for a hero once upon a time?"

Cory didn't reply. Kelsey's words struck close to her own daydreams. She used to wish for a hero. In fact, she used to wish for two. The brothers she never met, given up by her mother when Joyce's first husband died leaving her with massive debt, expecting a third and no way of raising two children.

The brothers her mother still had pictures of. Many times Cory had wished, yes, even prayed, that they would come swooping into their lives and save her and her mother.

Save them from the merciless teasing of fellow classmates about the secondhand and homemade clothes she was forced to wear.

But mostly, she had wished her brothers would save her from Zeke each time the court enforced the visiting rights that Zeke was awarded when Joyce successfully sued for divorce.

"Don't you think he would make a good hero?" Kelsey continued. "Those beautiful green eyes. Like a mountain lake."

"And about as warm." Cory grew tired of hearing Kelsey defending a man she had to see in a few moments. "He's a lawyer," she said shortly. As if that explained everything.

Kelsey held up her hand. "No lawyer, jokes. Okay?"

"But I've got so many good ones."

"So, how did you know him?" Kelsey said, changing the subject. "A date? He tried to ask you out, and you did your usual Ice Woman thing and brushed him off?"

"No."

"So. How?"

Cory hesitated, years of keeping to herself and keeping secrets were hard to let go of. But what would it matter if she told Kelsey about Zeke? If Matthew had found them, Zeke wasn't far behind. And if that was the case Cory had no reason to keep secrets anymore.

"He was, no, is," Cory corrected, "my stepfather's lawyer. And the son of my stepfather's other lawyer." Cory drew in a deep breath, going back to a time of her life she had tried to forget. "Thanks to the formidable team of McKnight and McKnight, I spent every weekend of junior high and high school with Zeke Smith. My stepfather. My mother divorced him when I was twelve because while he happened to be a fine upstanding member of the community in public, he was a devious, manipulative schemer in private. And a nasty one at that. Unfortunately that didn't change with the divorce. In fact, it got worse."

Cory stopped, her emotions getting the better of her as her memories swamped her mind. She clenched the steering wheel, her knuckles turning white as once again she struggled with forgiveness.

"Oh, Cory. I never knew that."

"So now I get to meet my stepfather's lawyer and find out what new torment he has decided to bring upon us," Cory finished.

"I'm sorry. I feel terrible now."

"Well, you didn't know." Cory turned a corner and parked in front of Kelsey's parents' home.

Kelsey turned to her, resting a hand on her shoulder. "You want to come in for a while?"

"No. Thanks. I have to meet this guy right away."

"Well, I'll be thinking of you. Praying for you even."

"Thanks, but you've got some strong competition," Cory said with a sigh. "According to Matthew McKnight, he found me by praying. So you're up against someone who argues with earthly judges for a living and talks to God on the side."

"He's a Christian?"

"Claims to be. Goes to church. At least he did when I was younger. Of course, so did my stepfather."

"Well, I'll be praying nonetheless," Kelsey said. "You take care." With an encouraging smile, Kelsey got out of the car.

As soon as she did, the front door of the house was flung open and a young boy of five barreled down the stairs, throwing himself at Kelsey. Kelsey's son, Chris.

An older couple stood at the top of the stairs, watching the scene with benevolent smiles. Kelsey's parents.

Cory rested her arms on the steering wheel of her car, watching with a tremor of envy. Cory had often wished she had what her friend had.

A home where she was supported by two healthy parents who loved each other.

Once Joyce had been strong, but for the past ten years, since Joyce first became ill, Cory had to be the strong one, had to be the one who made the decisions and, later, the money. It took a number of years before the correct diagnosis was made. Fibromyalgia. But all that did was give them a name for the debilitating pain, headaches and lack of sleep.

Sometimes the responsibilities could weigh so heavily on her, Cory didn't know if she could go on. Then her prayers became desperate. Somehow, God always found a way for her to keep on.

"And now you have to keep going again," she reprimanded herself, as she waved to Kelsey and pulled away from the curb. "You're not done for the day."

She spun the car around and as she drove toward the park, couldn't stop the sudden racing of her heart. Couldn't stop the tug of fear that she resolutely blocked out each day. The corner that Zeke Smith occupied. Permanently.

At times she would catch a glimpse of a man's profile, a swagger, an arrogant tone and the fear would come out of its space and twist through her mind.

Cory thought of Kelsey praying for her as she parked beside Matthew's shiny car. The thought gave her strength. If Zeke had already found them, she and her mother would need all the help they could get.

Cory shut off the engine, closed her eyes as she took a steadying breath, sent up her own prayer, then got out.

As soon as she straightened, she saw him. He sat at a picnic table, his tailored suit an incongruity beside the rough wood of the table.

He stood as Cory approached. The sun, filtered through the trees above him, dappled his hair and face.

Deep within her, Cory felt the same faint brush of attraction she had felt in the restaurant. Enemy or not, it wasn't hard to see why Kelsey thought he was appealing.

It was something Cory had fought from the first time she had seen him.

She could still do it, thought Matthew as Cory walked across the grass toward him, her hands tucked into the pockets of her pants.

Just the way she'd angle her head, that slightly sideways grin that wasn't quite a smile, and he felt, once again, as if he'd been measured and found wanting.

He didn't know why it should matter to him, he thought, standing up as she got closer. He'd known Cory since high school, when he first started working for his father as a student lawyer.

She was attractive as a young girl. Now, her face was narrower, her dark-brown eyes were thickly lashed. She was stunning.

As she came closer she pulled her hands out of the pockets of her dark pants and lifted her chin.

"Hello," she said, her eyes flicking over him with easy detachment.

"Hello again, Cory," he replied evenly. "Thanks for coming."

She lifted her shoulders with a graceful movement that acknowledged his comment and dismissed it at the same time. But as she sat, Matthew saw a combination of challenge and fear flicker in the depths of her eyes. Then just as quickly, it was gone. He could have avoided this meeting. Could have told his secretary to contact Cory. But some undefinable need to see her again made him want to do this in person.

"So what did you need to tell me?" she asked,

folding her hands on the table, looking anywhere but at him.

Trust her to get straight to the point.

"It took me quite a while to find you," he said as he settled on the bench across from her.

"My mother and I have only lived here for nine months," she said, her voice flat, expressionless. "Zeke hasn't found us yet. Either you're better than him, or he did all the legwork and decided to send the hired help."

Matthew held her indignant gaze. During his career he had held his own against hostile witnesses, angry judges and perturbed lawyers. Somehow this one woman always unnerved him.

Then, as her words sunk in, he realized that she didn't know. Oh but how could she have? He had a difficult enough time tracking her down.

Matthew looked away and rubbed his chin with his thumb and forefinger. *I didn't count on this, Lord,* he prayed, blowing out his breath. *I assumed she knew. How am I going to tell her?*

Matthew lifted his head, holding Cory's now puzzled gaze. He knew her well enough to know that with her, the direct approach was the best. "Zeke Smith is dead," he said quietly.

Cory looked at him, then blinked. Slowly. "What did you say?"

Matthew leaned forward and took a deep breath. This was harder than he thought. "Your stepfather is dead," he said, almost wincing at the harshness of the word. "He passed away three weeks ago."

"How did he…?" Cory's words drifted off as she lifted a hand and let it fall.

"He died of a heart attack."

"Heart attack," Cory repeated, looking away, pressing her fingers to her mouth. She closed her eyes, then opened them again, shaking her head as she lowered her hand.

"Though my father is the executor of the estate, we found out a few days after it happened. He was living in Wakeley, Southern Alberta. I'm sorry."

"We didn't." Cory just stared straight ahead, as if absorbing the news. "We didn't know at all. My mom and Zeke have been divorced for many years. How could we know?"

"I'm sorry," he said again.

Silence lay heavy between them, broken only by the whisper of the wind in the trees above.

Cory covered her eyes with her hand. "May God have mercy on him," she said softly. She stayed that way as time stretched between them.

In spite of the animosity that always flared in her eyes whenever they met, he wanted to sit beside her, to comfort her somehow. But he resisted the urge, knowing that Cory would rebuff him. As she had before.

Finally, Cory raised her head, her expression noncommittal. "I'm assuming you didn't come all the way to Stratton just to tell me that Zeke died?"

She was astute, he thought. As always. "You're right. I also come to tell you about your stepfather's will. My father is your father's executor. Zeke has named you as chief beneficiary in his most recent will."

"What did you say?" Cory exclaimed.

"Your stepfather left everything he owns to you." She just stared at him.

"I have a copy here that I need you to look at."

Cory ignored the papers he was shuffling. "What did he leave to my mother?"

"She's not named in the will."

"How he must have hated her." Cory shook her head slowly, as if trying to absorb what he just told her.

"I don't think it was hate," Matthew replied. "It was concern for you that made him do this."

Cory said nothing as she played with the ends of her dark hair, twisting them around her finger. "My stepfather was never concerned about either of us," she said quietly, finally looking at the papers in front of Matthew. "Everything he ever did was to show my mother or me that he had control. That's what was important to him. Control."

Matthew didn't want to argue with her. Not now. He was sure her emotions weren't stable. It must be a shock to her to hear about her stepfather's death from him.

He knew Zeke Smith and all he had done for Cory, a girl who wasn't even his biological daughter. Matthew had listened to Zeke's sorrow over Cory's lack of desire to see him and how he longed to help her.

So he said nothing, only turned the papers that she needed to sign toward her.

"So what happens now?" she asked.

"You look over the financial statements and the list of assets and sign that all is satisfactory. That's the first step for you. My father was executor of the will, so it's all in order."

Her dark-brown eyes flicked over the paper with seeming disinterest, then she looked back at him. "So how did you find me, really?"

"A bit of legal help. We had placed an ad in a

magazine that we knew all lawyers get. We got an answer from Nathan Stanley who lives here and who used to be an associate of my father and grandfather. It was an answer to a prayer,'' he said sincerely.

"An answer to a prayer,'' Cory repeated. "Well, it seems God has a sense of humor. I've been praying for the exact opposite.''

Matthew let the comment slide and laid a pen beside the papers she needed to sign.

Cory tapped her thumbs together, pulling in one corner of her mouth while she looked down at the papers. Then she sat back and slowly looked up at Matthew. "You know, this sounds too good to be true.''

"Pardon me?''

Cory picked up the papers, glancing over the contents. Then she laid them down. "I still can't believe that Zeke Smith is permanently out of our lives. You'll have to understand that this is a shock.'' She gently pushed the papers toward Matthew. "But I don't want anything from him.''

Matthew's mouth almost fell open. "Excuse me,'' he said, hardly believing what she had just said. "Are you saying you don't want to accept what he's giving you?''

"That's right.''

"This is most unusual.''

"Well, I guess there's always a first.''

"You might want to think on this for a while, Cory. I wouldn't make any rash judgments. Your stepfather's estate wasn't enormous, but it is still a substantial sum.''

"How substantial?''

Matthew almost laughed. Money always got people in the end.

Matthew turned to one of the pages and turned it back to her. "It lists the amount here."

Cory tilted her head, studying the paper, her hair slipping across her cheek. She pushed it away with a graceful motion, shaking her head. "Looks too good to be true." She glanced up at Matthew. "I know we'll never see eye to eye on who and what my stepfather was. But I have taken enough from Zeke Smith in my life, and not in the way you think. I promised myself years ago that I wouldn't take anything from him anymore." She waved her hand at the papers that still lay on the table. "I don't trust this. I don't trust him, and I don't trust you," she said. She held his eyes a moment.

"It's a legal will, drawn up by my father and witnessed. As far as we can see your father's estate is in order. My father should know. He's dealt with enough estates." Matthew couldn't believe what he was hearing, and he was angered at her implication that his father was a shoddy lawyer.

Cory just smiled. "Maybe. But I've learned the very hard way that with Zeke Smith nothing, and I repeat nothing, is as it appears to be. He had you fooled." She looked up at him, her eyes holding his. "I'm sorry you made this trip for nothing."

Then, without a second glance at him or the papers still lying on the table, she got up and strode back to her car, her head held high.

Matthew picked up the papers, wondering what he was going to do. His father couldn't move on the estate until the papers were signed, or Cory had stated how she wanted the estate to be disposed of.

He had to stifle the surge of impatience. His meeting with Cory had not proceeded as he had hoped. He didn't have time for this. He had come to Stratton for two reasons. To see Cory and to represent his family at Nathan Stanley's anniversary. He only had a few days and he had to go back to his busy practice in the city. And an ex-girlfriend who didn't want to acknowledge the end of the relationship.

Matthew watched Cory get into her car and back out of the parking stall, shock vying with anger at the abrupt ending to their meeting and her implied insult. What a stubborn, frustrating girl.

Correction, he thought. Cory was no girl. Not anymore.

If anything, she had become more attractive in the intervening years. And even more frustrating. Trust her to make what he thought would be a simple job, harder.

Chapter Two

"Zeke is dead?"

Cory held her mother by the shoulders, gently easing her down onto the couch.

"I just found out, Mom," she said. "He died a few weeks ago."

Joyce raised her hands, as if to do something, then let them fall uselessly into her lap. "I can't believe this."

"Neither can I," Cory said softly. When Matthew told her, it was as if it weren't real. Hadn't happened. Repeating his words to her mother, seeing her response made it certain.

Joyce took a deep breath, slowly inhaling, settling herself. "Then it's over," she said quietly. "The running, the looking back." She looked up at Cory, shaking her head. "It's over."

"Yes." Cory sat beside her mother holding her chilled hands between her own. "It is truly over." Then, in spite of her feelings for Zeke Smith, in spite of the pain and misery he caused her mother and her,

Cory felt her face tighten, her throat thicken and she closed her eyes against the hot tears.

"Oh, hon," her mother said. "Don't cry. Please."

"I don't even know why I'm crying," Cory sniffed, palming the tears from her cheeks. "I have disliked him for so many years…been scared of him…." She drew in a shaky breath, facing her mother. "I never thought I would shed any tears over him."

"It's a mixture of feelings, I'm sure," Joyce said, stroking Cory's hair back from her face. "Relief may be part of it."

Cory nodded, smiling at her mother in spite of the turmoil of her thoughts and feelings. "But it's not completely over yet, Mom. Matthew McKnight came to tell me that Zeke named me as chief beneficiary of his estate."

Joyce blinked, stared at Cory, then laughed shortly. "He put you in his will?"

"Not only put me, Mother. Left me everything. It's a substantial sum." She said the words with a measure of disdain, remembering Matthew's intonation. As if the size of the estate would make a difference to her.

Joyce shook her head slowly. "I can't believe he did that." She clenched her hands in her lap. "After all the things he did to you, all the tricks he pulled. The deceit, the maneuvering…all to try to bend you to his will…" Joyce stopped and Cory could see her mentally counting, trying to stave off another attack of pain. And when Joyce took another slow breath, Cory could see that she had succeeded. Her mother's fibromyalgia attacks made her tired and left Cory feeling utterly helpless.

Joyce turned to Cory then, smiling her reassurance. "It's okay, Cory." She lay her head back, closing her eyes.

"You should go to bed."

"I will. But first tell me what you're going to do."

"I don't trust Zeke's action. I told Matthew that."

Joyce smiled wanly. "You're right not to trust him. But I don't expect young Matthew McKnight would understand that, let alone his father."

Cory heard the rising anger in her mother's voice and stroked her arm, to try to settle her down. Matthew's news was causing more distress than he would ever know, she thought. It brought back emotions and feelings that both she and her mother had guarded and banked for so many years, and it was frustrating how easily those feelings came back. "He seemed quite surprised. Told me to think about it," Cory said, glancing around the small living room, taking in the worn furniture, the marks on the coffee table. In spite of all she knew, she had a moment of second thoughts. "The money might come in handy...."

"Don't do this to yourself, Cory," Joyce countered, turning to face her daughter. "Don't let him make you hope. He may be dead, but somehow he'll find a way to disappoint you. You should know that by now."

Cory nodded, surprised that she had entertained the faint possibility. How many times did she have to be disappointed to realize that anything Zeke touched would be tainted?

Joyce sighed lightly. "I still can't believe he's gone. This may seem hard to understand but at one time I loved him." She was quiet a moment and Cory wondered what was going through her head. Regret?

Sorrow? Her mother certainly lived through enough of both.

"You did marry him," Cory said. "I'm sure you had a reason for that."

"He was a charming man. He played that part well. And I wanted a home for you." Joyce stopped abruptly. She reached out, taking Cory's hand again. "You've been a blessing to me, Cory. I'm thankful that though I had to give up your brothers I was able to keep and support you. That much I can thank Zeke for."

Cory was quiet a moment, then broached the subject that off and on came into her mind. "Do you ever think of the boys, Mom?"

Joyce gave Cory a bemused smile.

"Once in a while I wonder where they are and if they are happy." Joyce ran her thumb over Cory's knuckles. "When that social worker at the women's shelter recommended I give the boys up, I was devastated." She squeezed Cory's hand. "But what could I do? Your father was dead. I had nowhere to go. No money. I wanted only good things for my boys. I just wish Zeke would have let me try to find them." She laughed a harsh laugh. "Of course I was so ashamed of what I had to do I told them I wanted the file sealed. I couldn't find them, and they couldn't find me."

"Maybe, if the will is real, we might have some money to hire someone to go looking for them," Cory said carefully, as if exploring the idea.

Joyce's fingers clenched Cory's as her expression hardened. "Don't, Cory. Don't even start hoping. Don't let that McKnight pull you into that. It's a lie.

If it's from Zeke Smith and the McKnights are involved, don't trust it. It's a lie.''

Cory held her mother's embittered gaze, heard the fresh anger in her voice and realized her mother was right.

"I won't, Mom," she said. "I won't.''

"We'll sit over here," Joyce said, stopping at an empty pew close to the back of the half-full church the following Sunday morning.

Cory let her mother go in first and sat down, looking around the church.

She was beginning to recognize a few people in the congregation from working at the restaurant. In the course of her work, she overheard many conversations, was pulled into some of the men's discussions on crops and commodity prices. At first she didn't know what they were talking about. She was starting to feel at home here.

Stratton, located in Northern Alberta, was a good community and for a moment Cory hoped she and her mother could stay.

You don't need to run anymore.

The words fell down through her thoughts, shattering them.

You don't need to leave.

It was over. The running, the wondering, the hesitant friendships that were made always with the thought that in a few months, maybe a year, Zeke would find them. And when he found them he would slowly once again begin his program of intimidation, until her mother's stress level would go up, her pain would increase. Their only avenue was escape. She and her mother would be running again, trying to find a safe haven. A place Zeke wouldn't find them.

It was done. Finished.

Cory swallowed down a knot of emotion, as she let the realization of the information settle in.

Zeke was irrevocably removed from her life.

Overcome, she bent her head, pressing her folded hands against her mouth as she slowly sent up a prayer of thanks, unable to articulate her feelings.

Thank you, Lord. I hardly dare be thankful for someone's death, but I am thankful for the release. She continued praying, then slowly straightened, glancing sidelong at her mother, but Joyce was intently reading the bulletin.

Cory raised her head, looking up as if sending her thanks past the wooden, vaulted ceiling and out into the open spaces where she often felt closer to God.

A shadow fell across her line of vision and her attention shifted to the man settling into the pew directly in front of her. Broad shoulders, brown wavy hair.

Matthew.

She clenched her folded hands in her lap and quickly looked down as the momentary peace she had just felt, fled.

It was as if the fear and anger she had just felt release from seeped back. She remembered many Sundays sitting with Zeke behind the McKnight family.

Why did Matthew have to come here? Surely there were other places he could go, other churches he could attend?

And why did he have to sit right here? Right in front of them?

She wondered for a fleeting moment how long he was going to stay. Was he not going to leave until she signed the papers? Was that his intention, to force her into doing what she knew instinctively was wrong?

Cory glanced sidelong at her mother. Her head was still bent, and she hadn't seen Matthew yet.

Cory didn't want to look at him, didn't even want to acknowledge his presence. And yet, like someone afraid of heights, lured against their will to the edge of a high place, she couldn't resist looking back at him.

He wore a dark-blue suit this time. The cut was impeccable and the color set off the honey tones of his hair. It's thick waves were controlled, tamed by a skillful stylist, she presumed. Matthew McKnight would never have to resort to cheap haircuts, or inferior tailors.

Cory forced herself not to finger her own thick hair, trimmed by her mother whenever it started to grow too long, tried not to run her hands over the skirt she had made herself. As always, around Matthew, she was aware of the difference in their economic circumstances.

And as always it bothered her that it bothered her.

Cory pulled the hymnal out of the rack in front of her with a force that made her mother look up with a frown. Then, as she did so, Joyce noticed Matthew sitting in front of them.

Cory saw her stiffen, saw her hand unconsciously press against her chest defensively. Cory touched her mother's arm in a protective gesture and in that precise moment, Matthew half turned toward them, glancing at Cory.

As their eyes met, Cory found she couldn't look away. His eyes aren't green, she thought foolishly with an insurgent beat of her heart. They're more like aqua.

"Hello, Cory."

Cory returned his greeting with a calm that belied the increased tempo of her heart. Then as she broke the contact, Matthew turned to her mother.

"Hello, Mrs. Smith."

"I go by Luciuk now," Joyce said firmly, her gaze steady. "My previous married name."

"I'm sorry. I forgot. Cory did tell me that. How are you doing?"

"Not well." Cory heard the disdainful tone in her mother's voice and in that moment felt vindicated in her own reaction to Matthew.

"I'm sorry to hear that," he said quietly. "Is there anything I can do to help?"

"I would think you've done quite enough, Mr. McKnight."

Cory saw a flicker of disquiet cross Matthew's even features. He nodded once as if acknowledging Joyce's comment. Then he turned around.

For a moment Cory wondered if she imagined what she had seen. Wondered if she was hoping he was more than she had always imagined him to be.

Then the service began and Cory's thoughts were drawn elsewhere.

She prayed for peace, for patience and understanding. As usual, she prayed for her mother. That somehow, they could find some equilibrium in their lives. That her mother's pain would be eased. She hesitated, then prayed a prayer for Zeke, the only father she knew. She prayed that she could forgive him. She prayed for his soul.

The service flowed on and slowly Cory managed to get drawn into the pattern of the liturgy, the songs that promised hope and an end to their earthly struggles.

But each time she looked up, her gaze returned irresolutely to Matthew.

Against her will, she remembered the first time she saw him. He was standing in the lobby of the government building that housed the small courthouse of Riverview. She didn't know who he was, couldn't have. He wore jeans that day and a blazer over a T-shirt and looked absolutely ordinary and absolutely arresting. When she came into the lobby, he smiled at her. She smiled coyly back, acknowledging his interest, her sixteen-year-old heart beating just a little quicker. Then Clifton and Zeke came in, all busy noise and bluster, pulling Matthew in their wake. Clifton took a moment to frown at his son's attire, Zeke paused to wink at Cory and ignore Joyce. When they settled into their respective sides in the courtroom, the brief moment between Matthew and Cory was shattered beyond redemption.

Cory pulled herself abruptly back to the service, angry that even memories of Matthew could make her mind wander from the church service.

Then the minister pronounced the firm amen that signaled the end of his sermon.

The congregation rose for the final song and as the notes faded away, Cory and her mother turned to walk out of church. She didn't look back to see if Matthew was behind her. She didn't want to face him again.

* * *

Matthew walked through the double doors of the church foyer and into the warm spring sun, slowly working his way through the crowd gathered in front of the church. As he walked toward his car, he caught himself looking for Cory.

Then he broke through the group and there she was, just a few feet away.

He resisted the urge to catch up to her, to talk to her. What would it accomplish except to get another glare from her? He'd had enough of that for a while. He could talk to her about the will tomorrow.

The wail of a child broke through the soft morning, and Matthew turned to see a young boy launch himself at Cory.

"Where's my mom? I hurt my a-a-arm," he cried.

"Where?" Disregarding her skirt, Cory knelt down on the pavement, quickly looking over his arm.

"Right here." The boy twisted his arm around and Matthew could see a thin trickle of blood from a small scrape.

"Oh, no," Cory cried in mock horror, shaking her head. She set her purse down and pulled out a tissue, dabbing the wound. "Press this against it, Chris," she told him. "I have to get something else." She reached into her purse again and pulled out a candy that she popped into his mouth. "That's good strong medicine to help your scrape."

Chris frowned, working the candy to one side of his mouth. "It's a peppermint."

"Oh, but it's a very special peppermint," Cory said dabbing the wound with the tissue. Her hair had fallen to one side of her face, her mouth was curved in a soft smile and Matthew was surprised at the differ-

ence in her. The hardness he had seen on her face
had melted away with concern for this little boy.

Then she turned to dig in her purse again and
glanced up. Their eyes met and she jumped, pressing
a hand to her chest. Just as quickly, the surprised look
disappeared replaced by a look of detachment.

Matthew felt a surge of disappointment at the
change. He liked the other Cory much better.

"Why are they special?" Chris's question pulled
her around.

"I—I got them, uh," she looked back down at the
boy's arm, "I got them from a store where everyone
always smiles."

"Ouch. You pressed too hard."

"Sorry, honey," Cory murmured, her head bent,
avoiding Matthew.

Matthew knew he should leave. Cory didn't want
him here, but now that she had seen him, it would be
awkward to just walk away.

So he waited.

"That should do it, Chris," Cory told the little boy.
She stood, brushing her hands with quick, jerky mo-
tions.

"Thanks, Cory. I'm going to find my mom and tell
her about your candy." He turned to Matthew, staring
up at him with interest. "Hello. My name is Chris."

Matthew smiled at the little boy's welcome. "I'm
Matthew."

"You should go now," Cory said firmly.

Matthew almost took a step back at the angry look
Cory gave him.

Chris only frowned, then with a shrug that denoted
a lack of interest in adult doings, turned and ran away.

"What do you want?" Cory asked, bending over

to pick up her purse. She looked up at him, her brown eyes flat, her expression guardedly neutral. "Why are you following me?"

"I was just going to my car when I saw you." He tried to suppress the defensive tone in his voice. "It seemed rude to just keep on going after you noticed me."

Cory fiddled with the zipper on her purse, then glanced up at him. "I'm sorry I snapped at you. You startled me."

He didn't know why he should care what she thought of him, but her apology lightened his mood. "Apology accepted," he said.

Cory zipped up her purse, then gave him a polite smile. "I should go. My mom is waiting for me."

Matthew racked his mind for something to say, to keep her talking to him, but his mind was blank. The only thing they had to discuss was the will. And he knew he wouldn't get anywhere with her on that.

"Take care, Cory," he said instead.

She glanced up at him, her expression enigmatic. Then without another word, turned and left.

Matthew couldn't help but watch her walk toward her car. It was older, slightly rusted.

Once again he wondered what it was that kept her from taking the money.

He realized with a twinge of regret, that he might never know. In a couple of days he would be gone and what reason would he have to come back. Especially given her resentment of him.

And why that thought bothered him, he wasn't sure, either.

Chapter Three

"Come for a walk with me while Mary gets lunch together," Nathan said to Matthew.

Matthew got up from the overstuffed couch, glad of the reprieve. He had spent the last half hour trying not to get smothered both by the couch and by Mary's solicitude.

Coffee and cake and squares and more coffee were constantly being urged on him. Each offer meant a struggle to sit forward to take what was given, then a slide back into the reaches of the couch.

He had been invited for lunch by Nathan and had gladly accepted. Sitting in an empty motel room on a Sunday had limited appeal. He was obliged to stay around until Monday, when the Stanleys had their anniversary. Nathan Stanley used to work for his father and grandfather at McKnight and McKnight. But Clifton's schedule was full, and his grandfather was ill. When Nathan had informed them of Cory's whereabouts, Matthew had decided to take care of two obligations at once. So he would be representing the McKnight family at the anniversary tomorrow.

The sun shone benevolently down on them as Nathan led Matthew through their yard.

"Lovely flowers," Matthew said, noting the colorful displays in the flower beds.

"It's taken me a few years, but I finally got the yard the way I like it," Nathan said with a touch of pride in his voice as he paused to pull out a stray weed.

"You did this?"

"Yes. In my spare time."

Matthew thought of his parents' home and the well-manicured yard. It was precise and lovely and well tended. But a hired gardener took care of it all. His parents seldom even sat outside in it, let alone spent time walking through it to pull weeds. "You actually have spare time?" Matthew asked.

Nathan shot him a wry glance. "Not all lawyers spend every waking hour at their office or the courthouse. God gave us many things to appreciate outside of our work."

Matthew acknowledged Nathan's comment with a nod.

Nathan opened the gate at the back of the yard. "Let's walk through the park. Mary will be busy for a good half hour yet. It's not often she gets to feed young men." Nathan slipped his hands in the pockets of his suit pants, whistling through his teeth as he sauntered down a well-worn path toward the river. "I like to walk through this park when I'm feeling stressed," Nathan said. "Did you know that walking is still the best form of exercise?"

"That's why Dad is in such good shape," Matthew

said. "I hate to count how many miles he does going back and forth to the courthouse."

"Does your dad still put in those crazy hours?" Nathan asked. "I remember when I worked for your grandfather, your father was always in the office before me and out after me. I believe he even slept there at times." Nathan shook his head, giving Matthew a considering look. "And now you're going to be filling your father's shoes."

"And mighty big shoes they are to fill," Matthew said, stifling a small annoyance at the sardonic tone in Nathan's voice.

"Your dad only ever wore a size ten," laughed Nathan. "Not that big."

Matthew smiled at that.

"He's just a man, Matthew," Nathan continued. "A mighty good lawyer, but just a man."

"Well, unfortunately I don't think I can keep up to that man."

Nathan shrugged, looking straight ahead. "Why try? What have you got to prove?"

"That I'm half the man my father is." The confession came out of its own accord. No one had ever questioned the direction of his life. Somehow Nathan's faint criticism of his father gave him a small out to express the frustration that had been building over the past year. "That I'm worthy to carry on the McKnight tradition."

Nathan tilted his head and slanted him a droll look. "And how much sleep do you get, carrying on the McKnight tradition?"

Matthew couldn't stop the bark of laughter at that. "I averaged about four hours a night the past month."

"That's insane."

Matthew's sigh acknowledged the truth of Nathan's comment. "It's also half of the reason I'm here. My pride made me think I could try, but I couldn't keep it up. Decided I needed a break."

Nathan stopped at a bench that overlooked the river and sat down, his elbows resting on his knees. "According to your mother, there's another reason."

Matthew lifted one shoulder in a negligent shrug. "Mother seems to think I'm pining over Tricia. Which is strange considering I'm the one who broke off the relationship."

"Tricia is your ex-girlfriend I take it."

"For about a month now. She was a sweet, kind, lovely woman. But it's hard to keep a relationship going on about two dates a month. So I thought it better if we broke up."

"It's no life, son," Nathan said softly. "God made us for more than work."

"'All hard work brings a profit, but mere talk leads only to poverty.' Proverbs 14," Matthew quoted with a smile.

"'All his days his work is pain and grief; even at night his mind does not rest. This too is meaningless.' And that, my son, is from Ecclesiastes. The teacher." Nathan added. "He goes on to say that it is good for a man to find enjoyment in what he does. That this is a gift from God." Nathan faced Matthew, his expression serious. "And are you happy in your work?"

Matthew sighed, hesitating. How could he answer that without sounding like he was either criticizing his father or whining about his lot in life? He was making money. Lots of money. He had a condo along the river, an expensive sports car. Paid for. But it felt empty because in spite of all his money, Matthew didn't have time to nurture his relationships.

"Matthew, I'm an old friend of the family," Nathan said, his tone encouraging. "I'm allowed a few indiscreet comments. I've known your father since he was just a young hotshot lawyer determined to make a difference in the world. I've known you since you were a baby. And as an old friend I feel obligated to say that I believe you're not entirely happy with your lot in life."

Matthew laughed shortly. "I don't know what I have to complain about."

"Being too busy, for starters. You look tired, you sound tired. There's no shame in admitting that you don't want to be like your dad. Or your grandfather." Nathan sighed lightly, clasping his hands between his knees. "I went through the same thing. Wondering what was wrong with me that I couldn't keep up with your dad. But you know what? I think right now, I'm a lot happier than he is. And I can't imagine your dad taking time to do this."

Matthew acknowledged the truth of that as he rested his chin in his hands, staring out at the spatters of light bouncing on the river. It was hypnotic and restful.

A young couple strolled by, hand in hand, a baby strapped to the man's back. Nathan greeted them by name and they replied.

"You're right about my dad," Matthew said finally. "Most holidays he took his work along to the cabin we had at the lake. My mother would help him. Made things difficult as an only child. When I was eight, I got asked to Bible camp. Soon I started going there instead." Matthew laughed. "Now that sounds like whining. I love my parents and I know they care about me. It's just..."

"Not the life you want for yourself," Nathan finished for him. "And it's good that you can admit that." He got up. "Let's walk a little more."

As they walked, they talked about inconsequential things. The weather, life in Stratton, mutual acquaintances. But Matthew felt as if a burden had been eased. Nathan was the first person he had dared speak to about the very thing that had been slowly eating away at him over the past year or so. He didn't know how he was going to work his way around the problem. Lawyers at McKnight and McKnight pulled their load. And as the son and grandson, he felt the pressure most keenly.

He just wished there was a way around it all.

"How far does this park go?" Matthew asked as they rounded another corner. The trees were higher here, arching over the path, creating a welcome coolness.

"It follows the river on this side," Nathan replied. "It goes all the way to downtown and past that."

"It's great," Matthew said, slipping his hands in his pockets. "Very relaxing."

"I thought you'd appreciate it," Nathan said with a smile.

They strolled around another curve. A young woman walked toward them, looking down as she swished a branch of leaves beside her. Even from this distance they could hear her humming a soft tune. As they drew nearer, she lifted her head, then stopped in the middle of the path.

It was Cory.

She now wore blue jeans instead of the skirt she'd

worn to church this morning. Her hair was pulled back, accentuating the delicate lines of her face.

Matthew couldn't look away even as the gentle smile on her face was replaced by a frown.

"Hello, Cory," Nathan said jovially. "Out for a Sunday afternoon stroll?"

She nodded, slowly walking toward them. She looked warily at Matthew, then back at Nathan. "It's lovely out today, isn't it?" she said.

"That it is." Nathan turned toward Matthew. "I believe you've already met Matthew? I understand that thanks to me he was able to find you."

Cory's glance skidded over him, then returned to Nathan. "So he told me."

"And how's your mother?"

Matthew was glad he didn't mention the will. At least not in front of Cory.

"She's fine," Cory said. "She was tired after church so she's having a nap right now."

"And she'll still be able to cater our function on Monday? The forecast is for warm weather. So we are going to take a chance and have it outside."

"Sounds wonderful. My mother is counting on being there."

"Excellent." Nathan turned to Matthew. "Cory and her mother do some catering on the side. They're very good. We were fortunate to get them to do our anniversary supper tomorrow."

Matthew watched Cory while Nathan spoke, but she kept her eyes resolutely on Nathan.

"I guess I'll find out for myself tomorrow," Matthew said.

Cory gave him a startled glance. He guessed she didn't know he was going to be attending.

"Are you going to be helping?" Nathan asked.

"Uh…just for the first half hour. I'm working all day tomorrow."

"You're not going to be too tired?" Nathan asked solicitously.

"No. No. I'll be fine." She favored Matthew with a tight smile, Nathan a friendlier version. "I should go. Have a nice day," she said.

They stepped aside for her as she walked past, her pace somewhat quicker than before.

"Nice woman, that Cory," Nathan said when she was out of earshot. "Hard worker. She and her mother just started their catering business a couple of months ago, and they're already getting quite a reputation. I imagine the money from her stepfather's will should help her business out."

"I'm sure it should," Matthew replied vaguely. He wasn't about to discuss the situation with Nathan. He still had hopes that Cory would sign the papers before he left. Knowing that he would see her tomorrow helped a great deal.

"It always surprises me when a woman like that doesn't have a boyfriend," Nathan said.

"She doesn't?"

"Nope. Can't understand it. I think half of the single men in town are in love with her."

"She's quite attractive," Matthew conceded, curiously pleased to find out that she was still single.

"Oh, she's more than that," Nathan said, giving Matthew a knowing look. "She's got a snap and vigor to her that catches your attention right away."

Matthew wasn't about to dispute the snap. He'd been on the receiving end of it enough times.

Nathan glanced at his watch. "Well, we'd better

go home. Mary should have had enough time by now.''

They turned around and as they walked back, Matthew wondered if they were going to run into Cory again.

The idea was appealing and confounding at the same time.

''Coffee?''

Matthew took off his glasses, and looked up at Cory who wasn't any happier to see him than before. ''Sure. Thanks.''

''What would you like for breakfast?'' she asked, while she poured the cup full, her eyes avoiding his.

''Brown toast and two eggs. Over easy.''

Cory's curt nod was the only indication that she heard him. He tried to superimpose the picture he kept of her talking to Chris yesterday on this grim-looking woman who listened to him and yet ignored him at the same time.

Yesterday he had seen the first genuine smile on her face since he had come here. As she knelt beside Chris, taking care of his scrape, Matthew saw the same side of Cory he had first seen many years ago. The part of her he only saw with Deirdre, his cousin.

Animated, genuinely happy.

This was the woman he wanted to see again. And that was what drew him to the restaurant this morning.

But he was dreaming if she would show that side to him.

With him she was detached, businesslike and efficient. He didn't know why he even bothered.

Without another word, she walked away, stopping

at the table of some men who had just come into the restaurant.

She was much friendlier with them. Spunky, Nathan had said yesterday. Well, she was that all right.

When she returned with his order, he tried to catch her gaze as he smiled. "Thanks, Cory."

"You're welcome. Enjoy your meal." The words held no inflection. They were automatic and, he supposed, spoken hundreds of times during the day.

It bothered him and some niggling sense of annoyance goaded him into asking, "Have you thought any more about the will?"

Her eyes met his, tentative and unsure.

"I've been thinking about it," she said, carefully. "But I haven't changed my mind on it."

He stifled a sigh, confounded by her stubbornness. "But, Cory, think of what you could do with the money. You could do something with your life, make it better..."

As Cory's eyes grew hard, Matthew could have kicked himself. Wrong thing to say, he thought, as she glared down at him.

"There's nothing wrong with what I do." Cory held his gaze a moment, as if challenging him.

Matthew held it, remembering what Nathan had said about the business she and her mother had just started up. "No, I'm sure there isn't. But you're an intelligent woman, Cory. I'm sure there are other things you would like to do with your life." He felt like he was taking advantage of her, using information she didn't know he had, but he wanted to get this job finished. He had work waiting in Riverview, and he didn't have time to hang around here until she decided what she wanted to do.

"So only dumb women work as waitresses?" she said, her mouth curving in a sardonic smile.

"Of course not." He couldn't believe she was getting him tangled up in his own words. He was paid to use words, for goodness sake.

"I just think that you have potential beyond serving people food. I remember that you were a very good student in school."

Cory's expression didn't change. "You know a lot about me, Mr. McKnight. But not as much as you think you do."

And with that she turned and walked away.

Matthew watched her go, shaking his head at his lack of tact. At this rate he would be leaving for Riverview without accomplishing his mission.

He had only today and tomorrow to hang around here. Then he was due back at his office where the work was piling up now, even as he sat. He couldn't afford to alienate Cory. If he wanted to wrap this up, he had to use other tactics. Try to turn on the charm that usually worked with the other women he had dated.

Like Tricia, he thought wryly. Tricia who, in tears, had asked him why he couldn't spend more time with her.

He dismissed that memory. Tricia was sweet and had been a patient girlfriend, putting up with dates that were canceled when a big case suddenly needed extra attention, when Matthew left for hearings in other towns and would only talk to her on the phone. He just had to face the fact that his life up to now wasn't conducive to maintaining long-term relationships. Late hours at the office and working weekends just didn't mesh with having a girlfriend.

He pushed the depressing thoughts aside. He had things on his mind. And right now all he had to focus on was getting Cory to sign the papers. Once that was done, he could put Stratton and Cory Smith, correction, Luciuk, behind.

She came by later with his bill and without another word, set it on the table. Matthew didn't even look up at her, annoyed that she could make him feel ashamed.

He had every intention of finishing his breakfast and leaving. He didn't have much to do today. He'd promised Nathan and Mary that he would stop by this afternoon and help them set things out for the party this evening. But that was it.

And how was he going to fill the rest of his time, he wondered? He'd never had to face that prospect before.

He finished off his toast, swallowed down a last gulp of coffee and wiped his mouth, getting ready to leave.

"Cory, Cory, look at my bandage."

The voice of a young boy broke through the muted hum of the restaurant. Matthew couldn't help but look up at the little boy running through the restaurant toward Cory who was waiting on a customer.

It was Chris, the young boy Cory had helped yesterday after church. He ran up to Cory, proudly showing her the bandage on his elbow.

Again, she squatted down to get on his level, expressing her admiration.

He gave her a quick hug.

Once again Matthew saw the change in her. Once again, he saw a smile soften her features.

And Matthew found himself slightly jealous of a five-year-old boy.

Chapter Four

"Matthew, would you mind moving some of those chairs over there? I know some of us old folks will want to get out of the sun. I can't believe the day turned out so beautiful." Mary Stanley pointed to a spot shaded by tall pine trees. "I'm going in the house to get something cool to drink. Why don't you join us? It will be a while before the caterer comes."

"I'll do that." Matthew smiled his acceptance.

Mary nodded once as if signifying her approval and then left.

When Matthew was done, he looked around the yard, checking everything one more time. Tables were ready for the caterer, chairs had been set out around low tables, on the patio, on the grass and in the shade of the trees that sheltered the large yard. Pots of flowers were scattered through the yard, adding a splash of color.

Matthew remembered his parents' twenty-fifth anniversary celebration. It had taken his mother months to arrange and had taken her another month to relax from all the stress of the organization.

He couldn't imagine his parents celebrating an important occasion such as a fortieth wedding anniversary with a simple supper and reception served outside.

And he had to admit, this was much more appealing. Thankfully the weather had cooperated, obliging the day with sun and the faintest breeze to keep any bugs away.

Now all they had to do was wait for the caterer.

Matthew checked over his khaki pants, making sure they weren't too badly wrinkled. Thankfully the supper was a very casual affair and he didn't have to wear a suit.

He gave the yard a quick once-over, then walked toward the house. The patio doors were open to the large family room but it was empty.

Probably in the kitchen, he thought, walking through the open doorway. He stopped suddenly.

Nathan and Mary Stanley stood by the kitchen counter, arms wrapped around each other, exchanging an ardent kiss.

He should leave, Matthew thought, yet he couldn't look away from the sight of a man and woman, sixty-seven and sixty-five, obviously enraptured with each other.

He was about to turn, when Nathan lifted his head and grinned over his wife's shoulder at Matthew. "Hello, there. I'm afraid I've distracted Mary from getting your drink."

Mary's head whipped around and color flooded her cheeks as she pulled away from her husband. "Oh, dear." Her hand fluttered over her hair, as she turned to the fridge. "I'm so sorry, Matthew."

"Oh, don't fuss, Mary. It's not like he's never seen an old married couple kiss before," Nathan chuckled.

But he hadn't, Matthew thought. Never, in all the years he had lived at home had he ever seen his mother and father exchange anything more than a dry peck on the cheek.

"No, I'm sorry," Matthew said. "I'll go and wait in the family room."

Nathan winked at him. "Your drink will be coming in a minute, I promise I won't distract Mary anymore."

Matthew nodded, bemused.

As he walked back to the family room, he couldn't help but compare what the Stanleys seemed to have with his parents' relationship. He loved his mother and father and was sure they both loved each other. Otherwise, they wouldn't still be together.

But in spite of that, he always knew that he wanted more from a relationship than what his parents had.

He thought of the girlfriends he had in the past. They all had what he thought would be the necessary qualifications for a good relationship. Most of them were sincere, Christian women. Good-looking, cultured. Tricia was the first one, however, that he had dated more than a couple of months. She had been unfailingly patient and understanding.

Their dates were enjoyable. They had much in common and never ran out of things to talk about.

Yet he always felt something was missing. If he had truly cared about her, he would have found time for her. He didn't know if it was a problem with him or his job or the women he chose.

Or maybe a bad combination of both.

"Here's your juice. Finally."

Matthew turned and took the tall, cool glass from a still-flustered Mary. "Thanks," he said, raising it to her in a mock salute accompanied by a smile. "And here's to many more years together and many more stolen kisses in the kitchen."

"Hear, hear," Nathan said jovially, dropping into his recliner. "Come on, Mary. Don't look so embarrassed. It's not like we've never done that before."

Mary declined to comment and instead sat down in a chair across the room from her husband, primly smoothing out her skirt. But Matthew caught the secret smile she sent her husband.

"So back to the grind tomorrow?" Nathan asked.

"I'm afraid so." Matthew couldn't help but sighing.

"So what did you do today?"

"Went for another walk along the river. Found a nice quiet spot and just sat there."

"Watching water is good for the soul," Nathan said. "Do you ever go fishing?"

Matthew shook his head. "No time."

"That is almost sinful, my boy."

"You should talk," Mary reprimanded him. "You haven't been fishing yet this year."

Nathan acknowledged the comment with a shrug. "I was hoping to do some this summer, but that's out of the question now."

"Why?" Matthew asked.

"I was supposed to get a summer law student to help me out, but she changed her mind when a city firm made an offer. Just can't get many young lawyers to come out here. So looks like I'll be working

McKnight hours.'' He laughed, but Matthew could tell the prospect didn't please him.

"Why don't you retire?''

"I should,'' he agreed. "I've made my money. I'm past retirement age. If that partner I had three years ago would have worked out, I would have quit already.'' He looked at Matthew with a grin. "I should sell the practice to you, Matthew. Don't you think it would be nice to live in a small town? And deal with people you know?''

Matthew smiled politely, acknowledging the question, allowing himself a few moments of "Why not?''

Because you already have a busy practice. The words jumped into his head, intrusive.

But it wasn't making him happy.

He didn't want to live here, in this small town. A practice like Nathan Stanley's would be a step down, a lesser position. No prestige.

But it was peaceful and living in a small town could give him something that staying in Riverview under the steady watchfulness of his father couldn't.

Independence. A place he could establish his own identity.

Matthew took another sip of his juice as the thoughts bounced back and forth.

"I think our caterer is here,'' Mary said, angling her head so she could see out the patio doors to the driveway beside the house.

They could hear the engine of the car. It turned off and a door opened.

"My goodness. Cory is here alone.''

Matthew couldn't stop the quick lift of his heart at her words, then quashed that as well. He'd be lucky to get more than three civil words out of her.

Matthew set his cup down and followed Nathan and Mary out the door.

Cory had the back door of the station wagon open and was manhandling a large tray out of the back, hampered by her skirt. Matthew allowed himself an appreciative look of how feminine it made her.

And how it showed off the curve of her long legs.

"Let me help you with that," Nathan said hurrying forward to take the tray from her.

"No, I can manage."

"Don't be silly. Where's your mother?"

Matthew could see Cory hesitate. "She's not feeling well right now."

"Well, then we'll have to help you."

"No. Please. You're hosting the party."

"So? That means we can help. Might even get some credit from our guests for those delicious smells I am smelling right now."

With a light laugh, Cory relinquished her hold on the tray. "Thanks. These are the cold cuts for later, so just set them someplace cool for now."

She brushed a loose strand of hair out of her face, and smiled at Mary as she handed her a tray as well.

Cory turned her head, and Matthew could tell the instant she saw him. Her smile melted away and surprise flitted across her face. Surprise and something else, something warm and inviting. But then her lips were pressed together and her eyes grew hard and Matthew knew he had just imagined it.

He sighed, but stepped manfully forward to help her take the rest of the food out of the car.

"Hello, again," he said taking another tray from her.

The only acknowledgment he got was a lift of her

chin as she reached into the car to take out a large steaming container.

In ten minutes all the necessary food was inside the house and Mary and Cory were ensconced in the kitchen planning out the evening.

Matthew and Nathan were relegated to putting cloths on the tables and setting out plates and cutlery.

As they moved back and forth, Cory managed to avoid him. Matthew didn't know why he should care but her distant attitude annoyed him. He was as human as the next person and her continued antagonism was getting a little hard to take.

He intended to call her out on it at some time, but the guests were beginning to arrive.

He mingled with the guests, introducing himself as a friend of the family. There weren't many people invited for the supper, about twenty or so. A few more would be coming later. Most of them were older, and Matthew felt younger with each person he spoke with.

"I believe our meal is ready," Nathan announced a little while later. He stood on the deck, looking down at the assembled people below. "We'll be eating outside so if you'll gather 'round, we'll have a word of grace and then our lovely caterer can bring out the food."

The guests all bowed their heads, as Nathan prayed aloud thanking the Lord for the weather, the gathering and the celebration of their wedding.

His words were muted in the outdoors, an occasional breeze wafting his words away, but as he prayed Matthew felt Nathan's utter sincerity. His prayer was a simple conversation with God and it gave Matthew peace.

When he had said amen, he paused a moment and

then Cory brought out the salads. Mary moved to help her, but Matthew caught her arm.

"It's your anniversary party. Mingle with your guests. I'll help her," he said, smiling down at her.

"That's sweet of you," Mary said, patting his arm.

Matthew didn't feel too sweet as he entered the kitchen. He was quite sure Cory wouldn't appreciate the help and for a moment he regretted his offer.

"What can I do?" he asked her as she bent over the oven, pulling out a pan.

She jumped and spun around, her hand pressed to her chest. Her cheeks were flushed with the heat in the kitchen and perspiration filmed her forehead. Matthew was struck again at how attractive she was, when she wasn't scowling at him.

But then she recognized him, her hand lowered and she pulled her eyebrows together.

"It's okay. I can manage." Her words were clipped.

Matthew was suddenly tired of her antagonism and her anger. "Stop trying to be so stubborn and just give me the stupid pan, already," he said. "I'm not going to sit in a corner and eat it all."

Cory set the pan on the stove and pulled another one out, as if ignoring him.

Matthew grabbed the first pan. "Yow." He yanked his hands back, shaking them. "Those things are hot."

"Of course. They've been in the oven. Heat transfer and all that. I thought a smart lawyer like you could figure that out." Cory glanced at him, a smile hovering around the corners of her mouth in spite of her sharp words.

"Different set of laws than the ones I studied," he groused, inspecting his throbbing hand.

"Did you burn it?"

"I don't know. Hurts."

To his surprise, she caught his hand in hers and turned it so she could see the palm. A bright red line was starting to show across it. But he was more aware of the warmth of her hands and the surprising softness of her skin than he was of the burn on his palm.

One twist of his wrist and her hands would be captured by his, her delicate fingers woven with his.

"Do you want some salve on that?" she asked. "I have some with me."

He pulled his hand back, astonished at the direction of his thoughts. "It'll be okay."

"Suit yourself." She reached into a box beside the stove. "Here's a pair of oven mitts."

Matthew took the bright-red oven mitts and held them against his tan shirt, striving for a light tone, trying to gain back control of the situation. "What do you think? Is this me?"

Cory looked at the mitts, then back at him. That hovering smile of hers was back. "Oh, definitely. Red is considered a power color after all."

"Then I'll take them." He slipped them on, grinned at her.

His eyes held hers and something intangible arced between them, an echo of what he thought he had seen previously. But she averted her eyes and the moment was gone.

You're just here to help, Matthew reminded himself, picking up the pan. Don't read anything into the situation.

They had to work quickly to get the food on the

table all at once, and he was glad for the distraction. They worked in silence, but Matthew sensed that the mood between them had shifted.

When all the food was out, he reverted back to his role of a guest and put together a plate of food.

It was delicious. The chicken crispy and spicy, the buns soft. A pan of meatballs in sauce was almost gone by the time he got to it, as were the vegetables and the salads. He hadn't thought these middle-aged people could eat so much.

"Excellent food, Nathan," he heard one of the guests say, his plate heaped full. "My compliments to the chef."

"I'll tell her," Nathan said.

Matthew felt a flash of pride for Cory and her mother and reminded himself to tell her.

He ended up sitting beside a friendly woman who asked him about his work. He decided he didn't want to talk about it. He was still on holiday and was loath to discuss what he did each and every day. Riverview and the pressure of his father's law firm seemed as far away as the equator.

So he asked the woman about herself and while he finished his food was regaled with tales of living on a farm and the changes that technology had wrought for her husband and her children who had taken over.

To his surprise he enjoyed her stories and found himself envious of her close-knit family and the way they worked together. He and his parents also worked together, but the nature of their business was vastly different. As was their interaction.

Soon his food was gone and he wondered how Cory was faring. He excused himself and walked to the kitchen.

She stood with her back to him, washing a big pot. When she had come, her shirt was neatly buttoned to her neck, cinched with the same tie he saw her wear at work. Her hair had been pulled up into a twist on top of her head.

Now the tie was gone, the sleeves were rolled up and a few strands of hair had loosened from the twist, giving her a slightly disheveled and wholly appealing look.

Matthew leaned in the doorway, watching her, again unable to look away. Her expression was unguarded and as he studied her, he noticed the droop to her shoulders, the slowness of her movements. She looked tired and no wonder. She had already put in a full day of work. Spending most of the evening on her feet doing a job that should have taken two people had to be exhausting.

She dried the pot and as she turned to put it away, caught him looking at her. Again she jumped.

"My goodness," she exclaimed. "Would you stop sneaking up on me like that?"

"Sorry," he said, pushing himself off the doorway and walking over to her side. "I just came to see if you needed any more help."

"Look. I've been hired by the Stanleys. You haven't. You're a guest. Go out there and be one."

"You can hire me to help you," he said with a grin.

"I can't afford you."

Matthew sensed the hidden reference in her words but chose to ignore it.

"I'm a bachelor. I do dishes for leftovers."

Cory just shook her head.

"Please," he asked. "All those people out there

are older than my parents. I've told all my jokes and I've listened to all the stories about the Depression.'' And he didn't like to see her working so hard, looking so tired.

She frowned down at the pot she was washing. ''Well if you're going to hang around anyway, you may as well bring in the dirty dishes.''

''Do I get the leftovers?''

''A couple of drumsticks, okay?''

''What do I have to do for some of those squares?'' He pointed to a pile of plastic containers.

Cory followed the direction of his finger, then looked back at him, that same not-quite smile curling up her lips.

''You have to dry the dishes.''

''Utensils too?''

''It's a package.''

''You drive a hard bargain. Deal.'' He gave her a mock salute and walked out of the kitchen, smiling.

Cory didn't want to look. She didn't want to watch Matthew walking through the guests with a tray, picking up plates. The evening sun seemed to bless him as he moved, picking up highlights in his slightly disheveled hair, accenting the angles of his face, the whiteness of his teeth when he smiled.

He looked relaxed in his cotton shirt, open at the neck, and khaki pants. In his suit he looked more official, more like a lawyer. Today he looked almost human, she thought. And just a while ago, their conversation had approached normal, lighthearted. It was the kind of banter that she easily exchanged with customers in the restaurant and never thought she would ever have with Matthew McKnight.

As she watched, he winked at one older lady and Cory saw her smile coyly back. What a smoothy, she thought, watching as he moved on and Cory caught herself leaning forward, following his progress. She pulled abruptly back.

Grow up, Cory, she told herself. He's Matthew McKnight. Lawyer. He talked to the judge the same way he talks to those people out there. And you fell for that same slippery charm a moment ago.

She gave the pot she was scrubbing another swipe and set it on the drainboard. What were you thinking of, letting him help you?

She turned to pick up the towel.

The kitchen spun a moment and righted itself as she caught the sink. She really had to get something to eat, she thought. From six o'clock that morning she had been on her feet, and hadn't had anything to eat since lunchtime. She hadn't figured on doing this function on her own. When she had come home and found her mother in bed, her body racked with pain, Cory knew she was in for a busy night.

A lone leftover bun lay on a plate and grabbing it, she took a bite out of it, wiping the pan as she chewed. It wasn't much but it would hold her until the rest of the food came back.

Whenever she and her mother catered, she usually figured on putting a plateful of food together from the leftovers. But from the sight of the empty platters and bowls that Matthew was bringing back, it was going to be a dieter's supper tonight. She wouldn't have enough to pay Matthew for helping, she thought wryly, scrubbing a casserole dish.

She should have stood her ground and not let him help. He was leaving town in a day or so and then her life could go back to normal. She didn't want to have him around, reminding her of the past. Daily she struggled with the fact that she had to learn to forgive and let go of past bitterness. Daily she prayed that God would teach her this.

But all it took was one sight of Matthew and she felt all confused. Anger vied with attraction. Fear with fascination. Just like it had always been.

"Here's the lot."

Cory turned to see Matthew set the tray with dirty plates on the counter beside her.

"I just have to get the bowls yet."

"That's good enough...." but Cory's sentence died away as she watched him leave again.

It was kind of him to help, but she didn't want to see him as kind. It was easier to think of him as Matthew, defender of evil stepfathers. Having him coming and going in the kitchen made him too human.

Too appealing.

"So, how do we start?"

Cory kept her back to him, furiously scrubbing the dish in the sink, frustrated with her own seesawing emotions. "Just scrape all the leftovers into the garbage can," she said. "I'll wash the plates as soon as I'm done with this."

"Gotcha."

He whistled over the clink of the cutlery and china. Cory wondered how he could be so relaxed when she felt as stretched out as an elastic, ready to snap. She didn't know how to react to him, didn't know what to say.

For years he had been the nemesis, the enemy. And now he was here, helping her do the dishes as if all the tension of the previous years, all the battles, had never happened.

Help me through this, Lord. Help me just be civilized until he goes. She didn't know if it was the right prayer, but knew that anything else would be false.

"All done." He set the dirty plates beside her and she didn't even look up as she drained the sink and filled it again with hot water.

"There's a tea towel in the box on the table you can use to dry the dishes," she said, pointing with her chin, still not looking at him.

He found them and came back. While she poured the soap in, he flipped the towel over his shoulder and rolled up his sleeves.

The movement caught Cory's eye and she glanced sidelong at him, disconcerted by the sight of his bared forearms, his shirt open at the neck. He looked casual, relaxed.

Handsome.

He caught her looking at him. "What?" he asked, taking a wet dish off the drain board.

Cory just shook her head, flustered at her foolish reaction to him. "I'm thinking of a joke," she said, retreating to humor as a defense.

"Spill."

"What do you call a smiling, courteous person at a lawyers' convention?"

Matthew was silent a moment. "I haven't heard that one yet," he said, his tone light. "I'll bite."

"The caterer," she said sweetly.

"I'll have to add it to my repertoire of lawyer jokes," he replied.

"Actually, there's only two lawyer jokes," she

countered, thankful to be on the offensive. "All the rest are true."

"Okay, enough with that already. There's more lawyer jokes than there are lawyers. Let's talk about something else."

Only there was nothing else to discuss. Their only interaction had been as opposing sides. He as her stepfather's lawyer and she as a defendant.

The only time they had met socially was at her and Deirdre's prom, and even that memory was fraught with overtones.

She blushed again, remembering how surprised and dismayed she was when he had come as her friend Deirdre's escort. Deirdre's boyfriend had taken ill at the last minute and Matthew had filled in.

Seeing him in a social setting had totally twisted around her feelings for him.

"Let's talk about your work," she said suddenly, feeling as if she had to take the offensive. "What else do you do, besides badger witnesses and cajole judges?"

"I don't spend a lot of time in the courtroom in high-drama trials," he replied, ignoring her gibe. "A lot of my work is pretty mundane. I travel and sit in on hearings and read a lot of briefs, file papers at court. Prep work."

"What do you do for fun?" she asked.

He gave no reply and Cory glanced sidelong at him. He frowned at the dish he held, then looked at her again. "I don't have any hobbies. I usually work until about nine o'clock. Sometimes I catch a movie. Sometimes I go straight to bed."

"What, no social life?" she said with mock surprise.

"Not much of one."

"Your poor girlfriend."

"Yes, well, that's probably the reason I don't have one now."

Cory was surprised to hear that. And surprised to find that the information gave her a little jolt as well.

She would have thought someone like Matthew would have no problem holding on to a girl.

"Doesn't sound like much fun," she couldn't help but say.

"I think you're right," he replied, his voice quiet.

His admission surprised her. Didn't sound like the Matthew McKnight who always projected an aura of intensity and dedication to his work.

"So, what about you? What do you do for fun?" he asked.

"Cater," she replied with a quick grin. She was quite pleased with how easy she held her own. As long as she didn't look at him too much, she could do it.

"No, really. What do you do when you're not working?"

She shrugged. Truth to tell, her life didn't sound much more exciting than his. Less, if she were to be honest.

"I like going for long walks, as you've already discovered. I like sitting under trees and watching the leaves get blown by the wind." She sighed. "I like reading and taking naps."

"Sounds delightfully uncomplicated."

Had she imagined that faint note of envy in his voice? Probably had. Her life was a dud compared to his. "Doesn't take a degree to do it."

"How did you end up being a waitress?"

Once again she had to suppress that momentary shame interwoven with her dealings with Matthew. She had always worked, she reminded herself, had never needed any handouts. "I started in high school and never really tried anything else," she said defensively. "Because Mom and I moved around a lot, it was hard to get anywhere in any job." Now why did she have to say that? It sounded like whining and her vague reference to moving gave him another question to ask.

"Do you ever think about doing other things?"

Cory's hands slowed as she looked out the window above the sink, thinking, wondering if he thought she lacked ambition. "I've often wished I could go back to school," she admitted. "I wouldn't mind expanding this business, either. I like catering."

"What would you study if you went back to school?"

"I don't know. Anything. Science has always interested me."

"Yes. Physics and heat transfer."

Cory smiled at that.

"So how come you didn't?" he continued.

Their conversation was doomed, Cory thought, her thoughts diverted back to reality. Her mother's health was a factor, exacerbated by the constant moving. Lawyers' bills from fighting Zeke that took years to pay made it difficult. Never receiving any of the money Zeke always promised them made it difficult. Everything came back to Zeke and she knew Matthew wouldn't see him in anything but a favorable light. So she took the easy way out. "My mother's fibromyalgia."

"What exactly is that?"

"A type of neurotransmitter dysfunction. Nice expensive word for you," she couldn't help but add.

"I'll file that away along with the lawyer jokes." He took another dish and wiped it carefully. "So what does that mean?"

Cory scraped at a stubborn grease stain, wondering how to condense the pain her mother suffered, the relentlessness of the sickness into a few sentences. "It's hard to describe. She has a lot of muscle pain, fatigue, headaches. If she keeps her life regular, we can manage it, but stress throws her off."

"How long has she had it?"

"Twelve, thirteen years now. It seems to come and go. It wasn't properly diagnosed until about five years ago. The doctor she was seeing in Riverview told her she was a hypochondriac."

Cory gave him another quick glance. He wasn't looking at her, concentrating on the dish he was drying.

"Is she able to work?"

Tugging her lip between her teeth, Cory contemplated her answer. "She's not been able to hold down a steady job for the past ten years," she said quietly, forcing down a feeling of shame. It made her mother sound lazy, something she knew Zeke accused Joyce of each time he came to pick Cory up for a visit.

"And you've supported her all this time?"

Cory was uncomfortable with his prying, wondering where he was headed. Wondering why he wanted to know about her mother now when he seemed to dismiss her so easily before.

"We've managed quite well. And I've never minded. She's made a lot of sacrifices for me, as well."

"And Zeke helped out, of course."

Cory pressed her eyes closed and prayed for patience. Back to Zeke again. "My mother and I seldom saw money from Zeke," she said through clenched teeth.

"But he had court-ordered support payments. Of course you would have seen the money."

"We saw checks, Matthew," she said angrily. "Not money. Checks need to clear a bank account instead of bouncing in order to see money." She stopped herself, knowing where Matthew stood on that point. He didn't want to believe anything different about Zeke than what he knew.

"Zeke really cared for you, you know," Matthew continued.

Cory couldn't listen any longer. "Don't," she said harshly. "Don't even start defending my stepfather to me. You've done a more than adequate job of that in court."

"But he did. He told me often how much he missed you."

"The only thing he missed was being able to push us around." Cory wished she hadn't started this whole business. "I don't want to talk about Zeke Smith anymore. He's out of my life and it's over."

"But it's not over yet, Cory," Matthew replied, his voice quiet, well modulated. "There's just one thing that has to be dealt with."

She hated to admit it, but he had a beautiful voice. A slow drawl that would lull the listener into thinking this was the most reasonable man on earth. Cory used to listen to him speaking sometimes, hating what he had to say, sometimes wishing he would use that same captivating voice on her.

"The will," she said with a sigh.

"If it is true that you have seen injustice at his hand, then see this as his way of making it up to you."

How guarded he was with his words, Cory thought. He gave them both an out with his careful language. "Maybe," she said.

"I think you should reconsider what you told me the other day. I really think you should accept this. It's a chance for you to maybe realize some of your dreams."

Cory swallowed, then took a slow breath as she tried to imagine herself expanding the business and working for herself—a goal she had put away for some years now.

"This could be a good thing, Cory," Matthew continued, "A final blessing on your life."

Part of her wanted to acknowledge this as right even as her more practical part still held on to mistrust of the situation. "It might be," she said quietly, setting the last plate on the drain board.

"I think it could be," Matthew said.

She drew in a deep breath, as if steadying the hopes that were even now rising in her. "So what would be the next step?" She looked up at him and as their eyes met, she felt the pull of his good looks. He smiled a crooked smile, the hint of a dimple on one side of his mouth and she felt an answering tug of attraction. "Not that I'm going to do anything, mind you. I'm just curious."

"I bring you the papers, you sign them and things get started."

"No surprises?" Cory asked.

"Not unless some long lost child comes forward with a will that Zeke wrote out by hand."

"Zeke didn't have any other kids."

His smile became full-fledged, his head tilted slightly to one side and Cory almost took a step backward at the force of Matthew's charm directed solely at her.

"It's on the level, Cory. My dad took care of it all. If you don't trust Zeke, I can tell you for sure that you can trust my father. He's a good lawyer."

She thought a moment, unable to fight off the idea that maybe Matthew was right. She knew Clifton was a good lawyer. Look what he had done for Zeke.

"Okay," she replied, fighting that breathless feeling that she was making a mistake. That she was basing her decision on a charming smile. "Bring them to the restaurant tomorrow and we can do the deed."

Matthew's smile faltered a moment, then he nodded. "Good enough. I'll bring them first thing in the morning."

Cory turned back to the dishes, her feelings twisted around by the change in Matthew's attitude toward her.

He was a lawyer, trained to sway people to his point of view. People with more education than she had been moved to agree with him.

She clung to the memories as if to remind herself. She reminded herself of Zeke.

Yet, she also had to believe that Matthew was right. That the law would take care of her.

And slowly she felt her equilibrium return. Tomorrow she would sign the papers, and tomorrow Matthew would be on his way.

Her life could get back to normal.

But could it after seeing Matthew again?

Chapter Five

What did he want from his life, from his work?

Matthew knew it wasn't this. He knew it wasn't spending half his evenings talking into a small machine because most of his day was spent away from the office. Then going home, falling into bed and getting up almost before the sun came up so that he could head straight to the office and do it all over again.

He stood by his office window, hands in the pockets of his pants. Below him the river meandered, now drifting behind trees, then sparkling in the spring sun. Since moving to this new office a year ago, he seldom took time to look at the view.

For now, his working day was over. In a few moments he would be joining his parents at a restaurant a few blocks from the office. He would have preferred to go to their home, put his feet up in his chair, but his parents wanted to treat him.

With a sigh, Matthew turned back to his now empty desk, dropping into his chair to tidy up a few last files. It had taken a week and a half of long, tedious nights, but he was finally caught up. And in that week and a half he had time to think and to wonder.

He couldn't put Nathan's offer out of his head. Couldn't forget the difference between the Stanleys' relationship and his parents'. Couldn't help but think it had much to do with the pace of their lives.

And he knew, deep inside, part of the attraction was the fact that Cory lived in Stratton as well.

Hard to know why she held his attention. She certainly hadn't courted it. And therein lay her charm, he supposed.

Charm. He laughed. Hardly a word one would use in connection with Cory. Definitely *straightforward* was more like it. When he had come to the restaurant with the documents for the will, she had signed them, made some brief conversation and then went back to work.

It was as if the few moments they'd spent together in the Stanleys' house hadn't happened and they were back to where they were before. She seemed only too glad to say goodbye to him. Was he really crazy?

He leaned back in his chair, thinking of Cory and their convoluted relationship, wondering if he was fooling himself if he thought anything would change.

The only times they saw each other was in the courtroom, in an antagonistic setting.

Only one time had they met outside of that. His cousin Deirdre's prom.

His mind slipped back to that night.

When he came to pick Deirdre up she had asked if he would mind giving a ride to a friend who didn't have a date....

All Deirdre gave him was the address, and it took

them to a run-down block of apartments. Plastic lawn chairs taped up with duct tape sat on a parched lawn bordered by a cracked and broken sidewalk. A piece of cardboard was taped to the window beside the dented, peeling door of the address Deirdre had given.

He hadn't imagined Deirdre's quick intake of breath, and he knew that Deirdre had never visited her friend at her home. And no wonder. If his aunt and uncle knew what kind of background this "friend" had, they would absolutely forbid Deirdre to hang out with her.

Matthew had to know what was up. "So, who is this girlfriend, Deirdre?"

Deirdre bit her lip, still staring at the apartment block. "Cory Smith." She shook her head. "She would never tell me where she lived. I got the address from another girl."

"And why wouldn't you tell me it was Cory?"

"I was afraid you wouldn't want to pick her up if I told you it was Cory. I know you don't think much of her."

"Where did you hear that?"

"I've heard you and Uncle Clifton talking about her. When we've come to visit." Deirdre looked directly at her cousin, suddenly much more grown-up than he remembered. "I like Cory. She's a good friend."

Matthew stifled a sigh. This was Deirdre's big night, and he had no right to lecture her on her choice of friends. Especially not when he had found himself interested in the selfsame friend he felt he had to warn her against. "I'll try to behave," he said with a smile.

But as he walked up the sidewalk, he couldn't help

but wonder how Cory's mother had let things go so far that they had to live in a dump like this when there was no need for it.

He took a breath, reached for the doorknob, but it was opened before he could touch it.

For a moment he stood face-to-face with Cory. But not the Cory Smith he usually saw. Her hair hung loose on her shoulders, soft and shining instead of pulled back in her habitual ponytail. Her brown lashes were accentuated with mascara, deepening the hazel tints in her eyes. Her lips glistened. She had always been a striking girl. Now her beauty took him off guard.

"What are you doing here?" she snapped, breaking the mood.

"I'm here to pick you up." He gestured toward Deirdre who waited in his car.

Her deep-brown eyes shifted past him, as if she were afraid to take her eyes off him. When she saw Deirdre, Matthew didn't imagine her look of horror, followed by dismay.

"How did she...what is she doing...?" She stopped, her eyes like twin darts almost impaling him.

"I'm Deirdre's escort," he amended, wondering at her expression. "She asked me to pick you up."

Cory closed her eyes briefly, biting her lip. "Okay." She lifted her chin, smiled vaguely at Deirdre who was getting out of the car. "Let's go then."

As she swished past him in a cloud of satin he finally noticed her dress. A bouffant skirt with a snug bodice topped with a filmy scarf. Scarlett O'Hara in bright pink. He figured her dress to be about five years out of style compared to the narrow sheath that Deirdre wore.

He wondered what possessed her to wear it. Zeke had offered to buy her a dress. But at their last court date, in Matthew's presence, she'd told Zeke that she turned eighteen two days before graduation and she wouldn't have to take anything from him anymore.

Zeke had been crushed at her implication and again Matthew wondered why this girl was so cruel to him.

The first few minutes in the car were quiet and then Deirdre turned to her friend. "I'm sorry I surprised you, Cory. I thought I would save you the trouble of walking all the way to school. Angela gave me your address. I didn't…" Her voice trailed off.

Matthew glanced at Cory in his rearview mirror but her head was down. "That's okay," she said quietly. "I appreciate you thinking of me."

Her quiet pardon caught Matthew off guard. And it suddenly made her a little more vulnerable and a little more appealing.

When they arrived at the convention center where the prom was held, a bevy of giddy girls descended on them, oohing and aahing over Matthew's car, Deirdre's dress and casting coy glances at Matthew himself. When Cory got out there was a moment of awkward silence, but then she, too, was drawn into their circle.

Matthew followed bemused, watching Cory's interaction with the girls. She was slightly aloof, yet obviously well liked. An enigma. An attractive and intriguing enigma.

The evening was the usual for graduation. High spirits and overindulgence. Matthew would have been bored but for Cory. He couldn't seem to keep his eyes off her, couldn't keep from watching her. Wearing that ugly pink dress, she walked through the crowded room, smiling, laughing and fully sure of herself in spite of the fact that she came without an escort.

Intrigued by her, he asked her to dance.

She turned, her smile disappearing, her narrowed eyes holding his and turned him down flat.

Matthew was surprised and annoyed to see the anger in her eyes. He knew she didn't like him but had thought that on this special occasion, things might be different....

He saw her off and on over the next six months. And against his better judgment, each time he saw her, he couldn't fight the appeal she held.

Then, without warning and without a word, Cory and her mother left town. Neither he nor his father ever heard from them again.

Until now. Until he found out from Nathan that she lived in Stratton.

Matthew pushed himself away from his desk, and his memories. He was already late.

His parents were already seated by the time he got to the restaurant.

"And how was your day?" Nancy McKnight asked as he bent over to kiss her.

"The usual. Answer phones and calm down hysterical clients." He nodded at his father who, in spite of spending most of his day in court, looked as crisp and fresh as he had when he stepped into the office at six-thirty this morning.

And the reason Matthew knew what his father looked like at six-thirty in the morning was because Clifton had been there before him when he'd arrived at that time.

"We were just getting ready to order," his father

said, nodding at the waiter who had come up to their table at his signal.

Matthew picked up his own menu and with a quick glance over it, made his decision.

The conversation became general as his mother asked after his health and hinted at his love life. "Tricia phoned the other day. She misses you."

Matthew stifled a sigh. "I'm sorry to hear that." And before his mother could start on a litany of Tricia's obvious charms, he turned to his father and asked about the court case he had dealt with that morning.

Their food was served and as they ate the talk stayed superficial. Matthew wondered how he should broach the subject of spending the summer working with Nathan. Clifton would be angry, his mother disappointed, so he figured he better work the philanthropy angle.

"Nathan Stanley approached me while I was there," he finally said in a lull in the conversation. "Said he needed some help over the summer months."

"That's what law students are for," Clifton said, lifting one eyebrow at his son as if asking what this had to do with him.

"He had one lined up, but she got a better offer somewhere else." Matthew poked at his potato, then looked his father in the eye. "I thought I could go and help him out for the summer."

The eyebrow dropped. "Why would you want to do that?"

Matthew held his father's steady gaze and decided the straightforward approach was best after all. "Because I'd like to try a smaller practice for a while.

Because I've realized that working in a large law firm doesn't appeal to me.''

Clifton said nothing, his expression unchanging. His lawyer face, thought Matthew.

"And when did you come to this realization, Matthew?''

If his face didn't show his feelings, his voice did. McKnight and McKnight was as much a part of Clifton as his marriage, his family. In many ways it was even more important and Matthew could hear his hurt.

"I'm not saying anything definite right now, Dad,'' he said, choosing his words carefully. "Nathan mentioned he needed help. I liked the idea of working in a smaller practice for the summer. It would be a nice break.''

"But you just had a break,'' his mother said, laying a hand on his arm.

Matthew smiled at Nancy. "I know, Mom. I guess it hurts me as much to admit that I can't keep up to Dad.'' Nor did he have any desire to. He loved both his parents, but he knew he no longer desired their lifestyle or the type of relationship that came with it.

"And how long would you be gone?'' his father asked.

"I thought I could help out until August. You could hire an extra law student...''

"Much as you think you can't keep up to me, I would need about three in order to cover your workload,'' Clifton said, ending his words with a slow sigh.

"You're a part of the firm,'' his mother chimed in. "You can't just leave.''

"I don't have complicated cases, Dad,'' Matthew

said, concentrating on his father. He was the one he had to convince. "Any one of them could be easily handed over to any of the other associates."

Clifton shook his head. "I don't know if I can spare you," he said heavily.

"It would just be for the summer." Matthew knew he should be more firm, but it seemed easier to work this one step at a time. Besides, he didn't know what would come of this whole venture. It was a risk, and he wasn't used to taking risks. He had never had to.

But every time he thought of Cory, he figured it was a risk worth taking. August would bring its own conclusion.

"Besides, it would help Nathan out. When I was there for his anniversary he seemed quite tired." It was a bit of a low blow to bring up the anniversary. His parents still felt guilty about missing it, but Matthew knew that with his father he needed all the ammunition he could muster. "Think of it as a service project."

"And what about Tricia? She will be so disappointed if you were to leave for three months."

Matthew shrugged. "Tricia and I broke up a number of weeks ago. She's not a consideration." And she wasn't. He thought more about Cory who he had only spent a few moments with than he had of Tricia who he had been dating for nine months.

"And you'll be back in August?"

"Nathan's law student was just going to be around for the summer as well."

"I see." Thankfully Clifton hadn't caught Matthew's evasive reply. "Well I guess we could work with it."

Matthew was pleased. He was going to go one way

or the other, but having his father agree just made it a whole lot easier.

Why was Matthew McKnight back in her restaurant? Again. She thought he was gone. However, there was one way to find out what he was doing here. Cory approached the table.

"Coffee, Matthew?" she asked as she stopped by his table.

He looked up and grinned at her, dimples firmly in place, eyes fairly sparkling. "Yes. Please."

"If you're back about the will, a simple phone call would have done," she said as she poured him a cup. She wished she didn't have that silly jittery feeling around him. Two weeks ago she had felt a sense of relief when he left and now he was back mixing her up again.

"I don't have anything more to do with it. It's in my father's hands right now." He tilted his head as if to see her better. "I'm here to help Nathan for the summer."

"Nathan Stanley?" she asked, feeling suddenly weak.

"Yup."

"For the summer?"

"Starting tomorrow."

"I see." She clutched the coffeepot a little too tightly.

"And I'll have the special," he said.

"Okay." She turned and hurried back to the kitchen, her heart doing double time.

"Hey, wassup?" Kelsey caught her as she barreled past her.

Cory skidded to a halt and stood facing Kelsey,

embarrassed at her headlong flight. "Nothing," she said, forcing a nonchalant tone. "I'm in a rush."

"Why? It's not that busy."

Cory ran her thumb along the edge of the order pad and shrugged. "I just…don't want to keep a customer waiting."

Kelsey frowned and leaning sideways looked into the dining area. A slow smile spread across her mouth. "Well, well. The inimitable Mr. McKnight is back. And my friend is rushing around just for him."

"Oh, knock it off." Cory felt a slow heat warm her neck.

"And she's blushing."

"Stop it," she fumed. "I'm just warm."

Kelsey gave her a considering look, nodding her head. "Of course. I'm wearing a sweater 'cause I'm freezing and you're warm."

This would get her nowhere but deeper. Ignoring her, Cory turned and walked back to the kitchen with Matthew's order. She had better learn to settle down if he was going to be here for the summer like he said.

And how was she going to get through that?

By the time Cory brought Matthew his breakfast, her cheeks were a normal pink and she managed to exude an aura of control. Or fake it, anyhow.

"Thanks, Cory. I appreciate the service," he said as she set the plate of steaming pancakes in front of him.

He glanced up and she managed a cool smile in reply, covering up the little bump her heart made when he winked at her. She tried not to rush away, as if she were afraid of him.

Then the door chimes jangled again, accompanied

by a burst of noise as the first wave of the early-morning regulars started flowing in.

"Cory, honey, how about some coffee?" called out one man, pushing his billed cap farther back on his head as he dropped into one of the booths along the window and winked at her.

Somehow his wink didn't have the same effect as the one previous.

"Be right with you, Anton," she called out, thankful for the rhythm of her regular routine.

"You're looking better and better, honey," Anton said as she poured him his coffee. "No man yet in your life?"

"I don't need a man," Cory returned with a grin. "I can manage quite well on my own."

"Oh, c'mon, men are a big help," said his friend, slipping into the booth and pushing his cup toward her.

"Well, Louis, you know what a man's idea is of helping with the housework?" Cory asked.

"I think I know this one," Anton said pursing his lips in concentration.

"Lifting his feet so you can vacuum," Cory said before he could remember the punch line.

"You're a hard woman." Louis scratched his head, frowning. "Some day some man is going to come along who is going to make you eat those words."

"Or at least come up with some better jokes." Anton laughed heartily at his own retort and Louis joined in.

"Has Bill at the back come up with anything new and dramatic since last we were here?" Anton said. "Seems like we're always eating the same food."

"Careful, Anton. The more you complain the

longer God lets you live.'' Cory grinned at him. "You come here so often, no wonder the menu never changes. Now, what's it going to be?"

They both ordered specials, the door chimes jangled again and Cory's day began. People came in and some left but Cory knew the precise moment when Matthew got up from his table. When he fished in his wallet for a tip. When he looked around the restaurant and caught her looking at him.

Don't blush, she reprimanded herself, looking away, keeping her hands busy with some idle task.

Then he was gone and she felt like she could breathe just a little easier. She hoped the summer would go by quickly.

"Most of the work is pretty straightforward," Nathan said, as he gave Matthew a tour of his office. "I thought you could work in here." Nathan pushed open the door to an office room that was even larger than the one he had in Riverview. "I was going to put that law student here, but I think it should work out okay for you."

Matthew nodded as he walked slowly into the office. Two of the walls were bare, painted a soft peach. The other two walls were mostly windows, letting in extravagant amounts of light. The desk was oak, he figured as he ran his hands along its scarred yet gleaming top. The bookcases matched it as did the chairs. The honey-gold colors of the wood doubled the light, making the office glow. "This is just great," Matthew said, turning to Nathan with a smile.

"The furniture is a little old. I figure if I hang on to it long enough it'll be considered antique instead of garage-sale merchandise.'' Nathan spun one of the chairs around, grinning.

''I like it a lot.'' Matthew glanced back over his shoulder at the windows. They didn't overlook a river, they weren't situated in one of the tallest buildings in town, but when he looked outside he could see the park out of one window, Main Street out of the other. It would work out just fine.

''I'll get you set up and then we can get some of the backlog out of the way.'' Nathan laid a hand on his shoulder as they walked out of the room. ''I can't tell you how much I appreciate your helping me out for a while, Matthew. It's been a real lifesaver.''

''It's been for me, too,'' Matthew said, thinking of the long nights he had put in the past few weeks even after he'd caught up from his holiday.

''I should get your dad out here some day. Maybe teach him to slow down a little.'' Nathan shook his head at his friend's folly. ''He's too driven. Too busy with things that don't matter.''

And Matthew had escaped that, he thought. At least for now.

''I think we better all pitch in and buy Mr. McKnight a cookbook,'' Kelsey said, dropping the box of sugar containers in front of Cory.

''What are you talking about?'' Cory picked up one of the containers and unscrewed the lid. She handed it to Chris. ''Here, sport. Hold this for me would you?''

Kelsey stopped short and gave Cory an old-fashioned look. ''Oh, give me a break. As if you don't know what I mean. The poor man has been here every day for the past week.''

"Well that's the kind of customer you want, don't you?" Cory winked at Chris and handed him another container.

"I think it's the kind of customer you want." Kelsey leaned her arms on the divider separating the counter Cory worked at from the rest of the restaurant. "And I think you like that man with the dreamy smile."

"Oh, let's not forget the dimples."

"You can try to hide behind sarcasm, my friend, but I've seen you watch him."

Cory said nothing, knowing that Kelsey would twist anything she said. Besides, Kelsey's words hit a little too close to home. Matthew had been here for a week already, and it seemed that she noticed him each time he came into the restaurant.

Matthew was good-looking, no denying it. But looks were always deceiving. That much she knew. And men would always let you down. That much she also knew.

"What's more," Kelsey said leaning forward, trying to catch Cory's eye, "I've seen how he looks at you."

In spite of Cory's bravado, Kelsey's words gave her a jolt. "My goodness, Chris," Cory said, covering up her reaction and ignoring what Kelsey said at the same time. "You are a big help. And look, it's almost time for your mommy and you to go home."

"Good try, Cory," Kelsey mocked, sauntering around the counter. "But I know what I see."

"You see what you want to see." Cory set the sugar containers aside and wiped the countertop. "Doesn't matter what I say."

Chapter Six

"Lift me up, Cory," Chris demanded, holding out his arms to her.

Cory ruffled his hair and pretended to stagger as she set him down. "You're such a heavy boy, you're going to wallop that baseball once you start playing."

He grinned up at her. "Are you going to be my T-ball coach?"

"Sure am."

"You don't really want that bossy lady for a coach, do you?" Kelsey asked in mock horror.

Chris grinned and laughed. "I do. She's not bossy."

"Thanks for sticking up for me," Cory smoothed his hair with a smile. Chris was such a cute kid. She really didn't have time to coach him, but she had gladly made time when she found out Kelsey needed a coach. Kelsey had done so much for her, making Cory feel at home, befriending her and Chris was very taken with her. She turned to Kelsey. "Did you find another coach yet? I'm not too eager to try to handle sixteen five-year-olds on my own."

Kelsey gave her an apologetic grin. "Not yet."

"What? You told me I'd have help."

"One of the mothers backed out. But I think I've got another mother willing to help," Kelsey added quickly.

Cory glanced down at Chris who was starting to frown. "You start phoning tonight, my girl," Cory said to Kelsey, smiling to cover up her clenched teeth. "Our first practice is tomorrow."

"I'll find someone. Don't worry." Kelsey patted her on the shoulder. "It'll be fine."

"I don't know anything about T-ball."

"There's not much to know, Matthew." Kelsey set his breakfast of eggs and toast in front of him and slid into the chair across. She flashed him a coy smile, her elbows on the table. "It's only five-year-old kids, so it's pretty low-key."

"I don't know anything about five-year-olds, either." Matthew frowned at Kelsey. "Why did you ask me anyhow?"

"Well, you're new to the community, and it's a good way to get to know people."

"I guess so," he conceded the point as he picked up the salt shaker. He salted his eggs, then paused.

"If you want to say grace, I'll be quiet for a while," Kelsey said.

"Thanks." He bent his head and gathered his thoughts. He didn't like to just jump into his prayer, but knew that God understood his situation. When he was done, he waited a moment, then looked up. Kelsey still sat there, still grinning.

"You know it takes a real man to pray in a public place."

"Not really."

"Yes, really. I know a dozen guys who are Christians but put food in front of them and they just dive right in."

"So give me your sales pitch," Matthew said, wanting to change the subject.

"It's pretty low-key."

"Will I be doing this on my own?" Matthew picked up a fork, wondering if he was crazy. He had no experience whatsoever with young kids.

"No. I've got another coach lined up. You can meet each other tonight."

"Tonight?"

Kelsey bit her lip and nodded. "Yes."

"But, I've got work to do. I came here to help Nathan...."

Kelsey patted him on the shoulder. "That work can wait one more night, I'm sure. Besides," she added with a coy grin, "You shouldn't be working nights. You should be out enjoying the vast and varied social life of Stratton."

Matthew laughed in spite of himself. "And T-ball is part of it?"

"Hey, baseball is very big out here. You have to start small, though. Do a good job with this and we'll have you playing competitive softball yet." Kelsey glanced back and got up. "I gotta go back to work. So we'll see you tonight?"

"For sure." Matthew watched her leave, still wondering how she managed to bamboozle him into doing something he had no experience with whatsoever. He turned his attention back to his breakfast. Since he had come to Stratton, he had eaten almost every meal in this restaurant.

The food was good here, and he liked the busyness of the place, the sense of community. This morning it was as full as usual, chatter and noise competing with the country music thumping out of the speakers set around the restaurant. He knew a few people by name. One of them was a current client of Nathan's.

And Cory worked here.

As he ate his eggs and toast, he couldn't help but look around. A group of truckers sat in one corner, a few families were scattered around, a couple of single men and women, some of whom he recognized already. Regulars.

"Hey, Cory, honey, my cup's empty," one called out.

"I'll be by in a minute, Anton," she said. And then she was hurrying past him, her arms holding an impossible number of plates full of food. With a smile she set them down in front of her customers, asked if they wanted anything else and then gave them their bill.

She was all politeness and business, yet Matthew knew with them her warmth wasn't put on, her smile was genuine.

Except when she dealt with him. Each time she looked at him, he sensed banked antagonism and it frustrated him. As a lawyer he was used to adversarial situations. It was what gave him his job. But he had wished for a little more from her. Especially after their time at Nathan's.

Cory walked past him, but didn't even spare him a sidelong glance.

He finished his breakfast, dropped some money on

the table and walked out, suddenly angry with Cory and angry with himself. It was going to be a long summer.

It was one general scene of noise and confusion, Matthew thought as he stood on the edge of the baseball diamond and watched the group of children milling around. Baseballs were flying through the air willy-nilly. Some children were trying to catch the balls, others stood around looking confused holding baseball gloves half their size, others were running around in meaningless circles.

"My team," he said, pushing his hands in the back pockets of his jeans, wondering what he was supposed to do.

Kelsey stood by the fence talking to another mother who was kneeling down, tying up a child's shoelace. Kelsey looked up and waved to him.

"Over here," she called with a bright smile.

Matthew pulled his hands out of his pockets, sighed and walked over to where Kelsey and the other mother were.

"Hey, Coach, glad you could make it." Kelsey pulled him by the arm. "I'd like to introduce you to your partner," Kelsey said just as the mother finished tying the lace and got up. She turned to face him and Matthew's heart sank.

It was Cory.

Her smile faded, the hand she had extended dropped and Cory whipped her head around to Kelsey. "What is going on?"

Kelsey held up her hands. "Matthew is helping you coach the team, okay?"

Matthew could see from Cory's expression it

wasn't okay. "Hey, if it's going to be a problem..." he said, quickly taking a step back.

"No, no," Kelsey said catching his arm, detaining him. She turned to her friend. "I couldn't find anyone, Cory. All the mothers are busy. Matthew said he would help."

Cory looked down, poked the toe of her running shoe in the ground, then with a sigh, nodded her acceptance. "Okay. I guess we're working together, Coach," she said forcing a smile as she glanced at Matthew.

"Guess so," he returned. He would talk to Kelsey later.

"That's settled then," Kelsey said, her tone brisk. "I've got a list of the kids here and I thought we could spend this practice just getting to know each other, work on some basics like catching and throwing. That kind of thing. I have only a few more minutes to spare, and then I have to head back to the restaurant."

"What about the rules of the game?" Matthew asked. "I don't have the first clue about T-ball."

"I've got a couple of books. They're on the bench. It's pretty straightforward. I ran over the basic stuff with Cory. She knows where the players list is and the schedule of games." Kelsey flashed them both a smile. "Thanks so much for doing this. I really appreciate it. I'd like to stick around, but I have bills to pay and payroll to do. Thanks, eh?" She took a few steps backward, tossed them a quick wave, then turned and ran toward her car.

"Coward," Cory muttered, watching her leave.

In spite of his own disappointment at her reaction, Matthew had to smile at her comment.

"Well," he said brightly, "I guess we should start, shouldn't we?"

The only acknowledgment he got was a curt nod. Then she was striding back to the bench.

She picked up a clipboard and walked back to the home plate. "All right, kids," she called out. "Let's line up and get to know you."

A few children stopped what they were doing, glanced around to see if anyone else heard. When no one else responded, they went back to throwing the balls in the air.

"C'mon, you guys," Cory called out again with little effect.

Matthew walked beside her, glanced at the clipboard with the names, stuck his fingers in his mouth and blew out a sharp whistle. All the heads came up.

"Tommy, Jasmine, Terena, Scott, come over here." Those were the only names he could remember, but the children he named, obeyed. "The rest of you can come, too."

"I had this under control."

Matthew spared her only a quick glance. "Of course you did." He looked back at the children who were finally gathering in front of him and Cory. "Miss Smith and I are going to be your coaches for this year," he said. "And the first thing you are going to have to learn is to come when she calls you or when I call you." He smiled to lessen the reprimand in his voice. How firm should you be with five-year-olds?

"This is just a first practice, so we don't have to be real formal," Cory interjected, kneeling down to get at their eye level. "And I'm glad so many of you could come. We're going to have fun, aren't we?"

The heads nodded.

"Like Mr. McKnight said, you have to listen when we call you. And my name is Miss Luciuk, okay?" She gave Matthew the barest hint of a smile.

Point for you, he thought as she turned back to the children.

"First off," Cory continued, "I want you to listen as I call out your names. You have to line up when we tell you."

More nodding.

Matthew watched as the first group of the children whose names Cory called off obediently lined up, then across from them, the others.

"Move a little farther apart," he told them.

Cory glanced at him again, then looked back at the children. "I've got it under control, Mr. McKnight." She turned back to the children.

"Well, the way they throw, I'm sure we're going to have a few bonked heads and a few tears in a moment."

"I said it's fine," she snapped.

Matthew knew Cory well enough to stop arguing but had to smile when she surreptitiously walked through the children, spacing them farther away from each other.

"Mr. McKnight, can you come here so I can show the children what we have to do?" Cory called to him.

Matthew saluted and sauntered over, unable to resist moving one of the children a little farther away from the child beside him.

She gave him a cool glance, then turned to their charges. "I'm going to show you how to hold your glove to catch the ball. Now I want you all to watch.

Make sure your glove is in front of you and tilted slightly back.'' She showed them the pocket where the ball was supposed to land, how to put their hands in it.

"Ready, Mr. McKnight?'' Cory asked.

He nodded and Cory pitched the ball at him. She had a surprisingly hard arm and the ball hit his hands with a stinging smack. But he wasn't about to let her see his reaction.

He threw the ball carefully back at her and she caught it neatly with her glove, showing the children how it landed.

"Now I want you to try.'' She handed them out and soon the air was filled with balls flying back and forth, most barely reaching the other line. Kids laughed and squealed and Matthew and Cory walked along the lineup, showing how to throw and how to catch. Matthew chatted with the kids, trying to remember their names.

But as he was talking with one boy the inevitable happened. A ball thrown awry arched through the air and landed directly on top of Sasha Thibault's head. She looked around, her large blue eyes wide, then she sat down and began to cry.

"That was a big bump, wasn't it?'' Matthew crouched down beside her and held her by the shoulders, smiling encouragement at her. "I bet that was a surprise?''

Sasha nodded and wiped her tears with a sleeve of her sweatshirt.

"Where did it hit you?''

She showed him and he made a big fuss about feeling the top of her head.

"There's no bump and your head didn't dent so I

guess you're okay." He sat back on his haunches, grinning at her.

"I guess so." She felt her head just to make sure, and then Matthew helped her up.

"Atta girl, Sasha. You're pretty tough." He patted her once on her head.

He looked up in time to see Cory staring at him. He frowned, wondering what he had done wrong this time. But her expression was bemused and he could see a faint smile teasing her mouth.

He winked at her, her expression hardened and they were back to where they started. Again.

The rest of the practice went by quickly, and Matthew discovered, to his surprise, that he was having fun. The kids were noisy and rambunctious, but for the most part willing and eager to please.

When the parents came to pick up the children, he took the time to chat with them, reminding them and the children of their regular Wednesday practice. He realized what Kelsey said was true. It was a good way to meet people from the community. He spent some time with Alana Thibault, Sasha's mother, explaining to her what happened. Fortunately she waved the incident off and thanked Matthew profusely for spending time with her daughter.

As the last child was picked up, Matthew turned to Cory. "Well, that went pretty well, didn't it?"

"What, the practice, or chatting up Sasha's mother?" Cory said with a wry look.

"What do you mean?" he asked, puzzled.

"Don't tell me you couldn't tell how she was flashing those big blue eyes at you?"

Matthew forced a grin, determined not to let her get to him. "You're not jealous are you?"

"Are you kidding?"

And when she bent over to pick up the stray baseballs, Matthew was surprised to find out that her easy dismissal bothered him. A little. But what bothered him more was her obvious antagonism toward him.

"So, McKnight, next Wednesday we can do this again," Cory said when all the equipment was picked up.

"I guess so. I'll have to see if I'm caught up on Nathan's work by then."

"Don't tell me you're planning on working nights while you're here?" Cory asked, zipping up the bag. She was about to pick it up, when Matthew took it from her. "I can carry it," she protested.

"Maybe, but my momma raised me better than that," he said taking it from her. He swung it over his shoulder and waited as she gathered up the clipboard and the books of rules. "As to your other comment, I had come to help out Nathan, so if it means working late, then I guess that's what I'll do."

Cory walked alongside him, silent for a while. When they reached her car, she turned to him. "You've got a really driven kind of personality, haven't you?"

"That doesn't sound like a compliment."

Cory shrugged, opening the trunk of her car. "Maybe not. It just seems to me that life should be more than working, shouldn't it?"

Matthew dropped the bag in the back of the car and closed it. Then he leaned against it and tilted his head, wondering why she was probing. Ever since he had come to Stratton she had kept herself aloof from him, had only spoken to him with tones of irony in her voice, or not at all. A few moments ago she had neatly pushed him aside. Now she was challenging him on a personal level. "Is this the beginning of a conversation, Cory? 'Cause if it is, then I'm allowed to ask questions, too."

Cory held his gaze then looked away. "You've asked me enough questions in my life," she said.

Matthew understood what she alluded to. "I was just doing my job," he said, careful to keep any inflection from his voice. She wasn't going to let the past stay in the past. Not even now that Zeke was dead.

"Of course." Cory went to walk past him, but he caught her by the arm.

"I don't think I'm too out of line to ask you what you mean by that comment?"

She yanked her arm back and to complete the affront took a step away from him as well. "It means that your answer is an easy out. Where is justice and truth and all the things that lawyers are supposed to be championing?"

"I was helping a stepfather who wanted to see his beloved daughter. Someone who was getting no help from his ex-wife." He knew it wasn't what she wanted to hear, but it was the truth.

Cory clasped her arms around her stomach and leaned back against the car, her eyes closed. "I wasn't as beloved as Zeke has led you to believe, Matthew."

"You've said that before."

"And you've practically called me a liar." She glared at him and then looked away. "I don't know why you keep coming back to him, why you keep defending him. You're not his lawyer anymore."

"No, but he was more than just a client."

Cory acknowledged the comment with a curt nod.

"Lucky him. Our lawyer just saw us as another chance to try to defeat the formidable McKnights."

"We weren't so formidable. We lost cases."

"Not against our lawyer."

"It was the judge who made the ruling. Your father had court-ordered visits. That was preestablished and not by me or my father. We were just making sure that it was done."

"No matter the cost?"

"To whom?"

"Me." Cory pushed herself away from the car, her face hard. "I was the one who had to go and see him. I was the one who had to put up with his abuse. Me. No one else."

Matthew kept silent. He knew that she required a stand against Zeke and for her. To choose Zeke would be to deny what she was saying. He didn't want to do that. Yet, to deny Zeke would be to acknowledge that he had been wrong those years. And he *couldn't* do that.

"So now you see why we can't really have a conversation, don't you?" Cory continued. Her shoulders slumped and she turned back to her car to open the door.

"Why does Zeke even have to come up? Surely we can get to know each other apart from him?"

Cory shook her head. "I don't see how."

"He's gone. It's over."

Cory fiddled with her keys, then looked up at him, her expression sorrowful. "Maybe. But the reality is my mother and I are still living with the repercussions. I don't think it will ever be over." She got in the car and drove away.

Matthew watched her go, his hands planted on his

hips, puzzled. He hadn't thought she was a vindictive woman, yet her tenacity in her dislike of Zeke didn't seem to fit with the other glimpses he got of her. And it was going to be challenging in the coming months to meld all the different impressions he had of this puzzling woman.

Chapter Seven

"**W**hat in the world were you thinking of?" Cory shut the door to the restaurant's office and stood facing Kelsey, her arms clasped tightly across her chest. "You led me to believe I'd be coaching with another mother."

"No, I didn't. I said I would get you some help." Kelsey leaned back from her desk, pushing her unruly hair back from her face as she grinned at her friend. "And I did. I think it's a really good idea to have a guy helping you with all those kids."

"Not Matthew McKnight."

Kelsey just smiled.

"And you can forget that 'methinks thou dost protest too strongly' stuff you like applying to him and me," Cory said.

Kelsey just shrugged.

Cory tried glaring harder, then placed her hands palms down on the desk, leaning closer. "You have to find someone else, either to replace him or me."

With a sigh, Kelsey straightened. "You can't go

because Chris is counting on you to be there. And trust me, Cory, I went through the Stratton phone book starting at *A* trying to find someone who could help out. Matthew was a last resort."

"I don't know if I can work with him."

"Chris really likes him. He's a decent guy, Cory. Besides, it's only for a while."

Cory bit her lip and looked away. Everything surrounding Matthew was "only for a while."

Yesterday had been difficult, pretending nothing had ever happened between them. But all those years of frustration and anger didn't disappear in a few days.

Help me get past this, Lord, she prayed, *I don't like feeling this confused.*

"This is really a problem, isn't it?"

"Yes. Well, and no."

"It's not just your stepfather, is it?"

Cory shrugged.

"Talk to me, Cory," Kelsey said leaning forward. "I'm your friend. I've prayed for you, and you know that I care what happens to you."

Cory smiled as she held Kelsey's sincere gaze, conceding that she was right. So she dropped into a chair across the desk and tried to explain. "He just makes me feel so confused and frustrated. That's all. I feel like I shouldn't have signed that will. I feel like I've gone against my principles. My mom keeps ragging on about how she doesn't trust any of it. I'm just all mixed-up."

"You know, Cory, you can get yourself all tangled up in the right and wrong of this, or you can let go of all that stuff you're carrying around. Next time you plan to talk to God, let Him help you with this. Let

Him take care of it.'' Kelsey rested her chin on her hands, her expression thoughtful. ''You don't have to solve this on your own. But I don't think it's fair of you to take all the sorrows of your life and dump them on Matthew McKnight's shoulders.''

Cory pressed her hands against her face and shook her head. ''I know, but it sounds too easy.'' There was more, but she didn't even want to acknowledge her attraction to Matthew to herself, let alone her friend.

''It isn't easy, but it doesn't have to be as hard as you're making it.'' Kelsey got up and walked around the desk to kneel at Cory's side. ''Matthew is a really nice guy. And whether you want to admit it or not, I think he likes you too.''

''Oh, please. Don't start on that.'' Cory didn't want to hear that. It just added to the problem.

''Look, if you really want, I can try to find someone else. Maybe twist one of the mother's arms. Some of them hang around for the practice anyhow, maybe they can help out.''

''No. You're right. I should be more mature.'' Cory rubbed her forehead with an index finger, as if trying to force away her agitation.

''Well, you have to admit, he's easy on the eyes. You can't fault me for that,'' Kelsey said with a laugh as she got up.

''No, I can't,'' Cory admitted. And that was the closest she dared venture to part of how she really felt about Matthew McKnight.

''Let go of all that past stuff,'' Kelsey said. ''Try to treat him like you've never met him before, like he's an ordinary guy. It will make your summer a lot more pleasant.''

Cory admitted the truth of Kelsey's words. Even though she knew she could never truly get past everything that happened, she realized that it would be far easier on her if she followed Kelsey's advice.

Matthew bit his lip, glanced one more time at the telephone and then made the phone call before he changed his mind.

Kelsey picked it up on the first ring.

"Hi, Kelsey. I need to talk to you."

"Oh, no," he heard her say. "Don't tell me you're going to ask to quit, too?"

"What do you mean, too?" He picked up a pencil and began doodling on a notepad in front of him.

"Cory was just in my office, asking if she could quit. Honestly! You two! This is not the major leagues. It's some poor five-year-olds who want to have fun."

It wasn't hard to hear the frustration in her voice. Matthew felt sorry for her and realized how petty he was being.

"Well, I'll admit that it had crossed my mind, but the thought is gone now."

"Good." Kelsey's voice became brisk and animated and for a moment Matthew felt as if he'd been had. "Because to tell you the truth, Matthew, I think the lady likes you and doesn't want to admit it."

"You're really a dreamer, aren't you?" Matthew laughed shortly.

"Nope. I just know how to read people. Trust me, Matthew, Cory isn't all prickles and stings. She just likes to act that way because it's easier."

Matthew smiled and doodled some more. "Easier than what?"

"Letting people get close to her. You know, Matthew, I don't know much about her, but I do know she's had lots of pain and disappointment in her life. I really, really like her and I want good things for her."

Matthew leaned back in his chair. Kelsey's defense of Cory was surprising and yet not. He remembered Deirdre telling him that he had read Cory all wrong as well. Cory seemed to inspire a fierce devotion in the people who knew her. "So what do you want me to do?"

"Try to find out her side of the story. For her sake. She told me once that no one would listen to her. Maybe you should."

Matthew sighed, remembering his dilemma yesterday. Zeke or Cory. Who was telling the truth? Believing Zeke justified his own actions. But to disbelieve Cory was a barrier to getting to know her better.

And he knew that right now, that was something he wanted.

"Just listen to her," Kelsey urged again.

"Thanks for the advice, Kelsey," Matthew said, encouraged by the phone call. "I'll try to see if I can follow it."

"Run after the ball, Sasha. It's getting away from you," Cory called out, laughing as the little girl looked up from her study of her baseball glove, her expression one of confusion. "It's behind you, dear," Cory encouraged. "You need to get it and throw it to first base."

Sasha tilted her head back, then faced Cory. "I don't see it."

"You have to turn right around," Matthew called out. But little Stephen had come running in from his position at shortstop, pounced on it and threw it by the time Sasha realized she had to look a little farther.

The little boy on first caught it but by that time, the batter had plenty of time to amble to first base.

Matthew walked over to Sasha and knelt on one knee. Cory couldn't hear what he said, but as he talked he pointed to the batter, then first base. His expression was intent, and Cory knew that Sasha was getting a little more information than she had bargained for.

He straightened, patted her on the head and sauntered back, a light grin tugging on his mouth.

Easy on the eye, all right, Cory thought, watching him. In faded blue jeans and a baggy T-shirt with the sleeves torn off, he was that. Easy on the eyes and somehow less the Matthew she had spent so much time disliking.

She couldn't help remember what Kelsey had told her. Was she really making more of this than she had to? It was just that her relationship with Matthew, if she wanted to call it that, had never been straightforward. Ever.

But Zeke was gone. She and her mother had a chance at a new start. If ever there was a time to let go, surely it should be now.

"Got her all straightened out?" she asked, forcing a teasing note into her voice.

Matthew glanced at her, his mouth lifting in a careful smile as if he didn't quite know what to make of her.

And no wonder, thought Cory. One week she was snapping at him, the next she was bantering with him.

"She'll be in the pennant race yet," he returned.

Encouraged by his reply, Cory took a chance. "Matthew, about last practice…" she paused, uncertain of exactly what to say. "I just want to say that I'm sorry I was so blunt."

"Truthful, is probably more like it," he returned.

"Maybe. But I've been thinking about what I said to you. I guess I just have to learn to get past this."

"Does this mean we're allowed to have conversations?"

Cory laughed, surprised that he could be so forgiving and thankful for it. "I guess so."

"Good. Then we'll talk again."

His words hung between them like a promise. But it still made Cory feel uneasy.

The next boy, Scott, went up to bat, hit the ball squarely and once again it rolled past Sasha who, this time, was intently watching the vapor trail of a jet overhead.

"So much for Most Valuable Player," Matthew sighed as once again he walked over to explain to Sasha what she had to do.

Cory laughed, picking up a stray helmet. "Jay. It's your turn up to bat," she called out.

Thankfully the next few balls sailed into left field. Which was a good thing because Sasha was alternately inspecting her glove or crouched down, analyzing the grass.

Cory stayed with the batters; Matthew worked with the kids in the field. Her job was easy compared to his. She just had to show them how to hit the ball. He was busy running from one child to the other, explaining where they had to throw the ball and why.

"But it's too far to throw it to first base," one girl complained. So he moved her to second base.

"How come she gets to play second? I wanted to," another boy whined.

"No complaining," Matthew said sternly, "or I'm going to get Coach Luciuk to come and talk to you."

"Hey," Cory called out. "How come I have to be the heavy?"

Matthew looked up at her and even from this distance she could see his wink. "Because you're bossier than I am."

"Since when?"

"Since you made me dry dishes for a couple of squares," he returned.

Cory laughed at that, remembering their conversation in the Stanleys' kitchen. She shook her head, still grinning, then turned to the little girl who needed help getting her helmet on.

The practice stumbled on but by the end, most of the children seemed to get the basic idea of what was expected.

A few mothers stopped by to pick up their children and after a few more rounds, Cory called out for the kids to come to home plate.

"Okay, you guys did real good," she said as they gathered around her. "We're going to have another practice next week and after that our first real game."

Thirteen pairs of eyes got wide. "Against who?"

Cory glanced at her clipboard. "It's a team from across town. The Eastside Eagles."

"What's our name?" one of the kids called out.

"The Westside Whiners," Matthew muttered.

"Our name is the Stratton Tigers," she said ignoring Matthew's comment.

"Oh, good. Top of the food chain," Matthew said.

She stifled a laugh, then turned to him, forcing a frown. "Would you cut it out?"

He smirked back and as their eyes held, Cory found she couldn't look away, couldn't break the connection. Matthew's expression became serious and it seemed as if he leaned a little closer.

Swallowing, she forced her gaze back to her clipboard, bewildered at how quickly her feelings could change. It was one thing to establish a kind of truce between them. It was quite another to let anything further develop.

"I, uh, want everyone here next week, ready to play." She looked around at their team who were all watching her. "You can go now."

With a whoop the boys ran toward their parents, the girls following more sedately.

"Well, that went pretty good," Matthew said, tossing a ball from one hand to the other. "I think they're getting the hang of it."

"No. It's thanks to your coaching," Cory admitted. She dared a quick glance at him and was rewarded with a cheeky grin.

"Wow. A compliment from Cory." His dimple winked back at her.

"I don't give them out very easily, so enjoy it while you can," she replied, seeking the teasing tone she hoped would determine how they got along the next few weeks.

They were done cleaning up, the bags went into the back of Cory's car and once again they were standing together.

A light breeze picked up Matthew's hair, teasing it around his face. He stood in front of her, his hands in the back pockets of his blue jeans, his head tilted to one side, as if studying her.

"Do you come with a manual, Cory?" he asked suddenly.

"What?"

"You know, some kind of instruction kit that lets people know how you work, what makes you tick? I can't seem to figure you out."

"There's not much to figure." She was unsure of where he was going. She hadn't dated enough men to feel comfortable with the slightly flirtatious tone in his voice and was having a hard time navigating this new territory.

"Sure there is. You can come across as so tough, yet when I see you with these little kids, I see someone else. When you're in the restaurant you can laugh and joke with people. And when I see you in church, you can seem so serene. Yet around me you are as wound up as a spring."

She swallowed. Wished he would stop talking like this. "Well, I guess I'm a lot of different people in one convenient package," she said with a forced laugh.

"I'm sure you kept your boyfriends wondering, too."

"Not really." She looked up at him. "Never had a lot of them."

Matthew looked skeptical. "Right." He leaned against the car, his pose entirely casual, but the movement brought him closer to her, made it seem as if he surrounded her.

"Serious." She took a steadying breath, uncomfortable with his nearness. "We moved around a lot, my mom and me. Hard to keep a boyfriend under those circumstances.''

''And the moving was because of Zeke?''

Not him again. *Please, Lord.* Not when she had been trying hard to see Matthew as separate from the past. ''Yes,'' she said quietly.

''Why?''

Okay, Lord, help me through this, Cory prayed. She had thought to keep Zeke out of any conversation they had but in spite of her resolve he came up. Again and again.

''Doesn't matter,'' she said quickly.

Matthew said nothing, his eyes still on her. She tried not to look at him. He was engaging, good-looking, and if she allowed him closer, she would have no defenses against him.

In spite of her conversation with Kelsey, the last thing she wanted was to end up like her mother. Enthralled with a man and unable to see what he was before it was too late.

''What's wrong, Cory?''

''Nothing. Nothing at all.''

He grinned, lolling against her car, his one foot crossed over the other. He was self-confident, in charge.

''So do you have time to go out once in a while?''

Cory's head snapped up at that, unable to stop the surge of her heart at his carefully worded question. ''What do you mean?''

''I have a few papers that my father needs signed. I thought instead of trying to do this at picnic tables or in the coffee shop when you are always running around, maybe we could go out for supper and do it there.''

"Business then."

"Absolutely. Besides, you owe me."

"What do you mean?" she asked, suddenly wary.

"Do you remember your prom?"

It was years ago, but she could conjure up the memory in a heartbeat. The ugly dress her mother had found in a thrift shop, the patronizing smirks from her friends. She wasn't going to go, but Deirdre convinced her to. But to see Matthew at the door of their apartment to pick her up was the final humiliation.

"I remember it all too well," she said, her voice brittle.

"I asked you to dance and you turned me down flat. I never did find out why. So I thought maybe if I took you out to supper, you could tell me."

"Okay." This was really going back, she thought. "Just tell me where and when."

"This Friday. At the Inn."

"Why not at the restaurant?"

Matthew shook his head, frowning. "Are you kidding? You'd be getting up, pouring coffee and before I know it you're walking around telling terrible jokes to the other customers. No. I want to take you someplace you can be served for a change."

She wanted to refuse. It would create a complication she didn't need. And yet avoidance seemed a coward's response. Kelsey was right. She had to learn to get past her mixed-up feelings for Matthew and the best way for that to happen was to simply talk to him.

"What time?" she asked.

"I'll pick you up at seven."

"No, you won't."

"What?" Matthew straightened, frowning.

"I'll meet you there."

"You will not. I'll pick you up. At seven."

"Sorry. I'll meet you there at seven." The last thing she needed was for her mother to know that she was going out for supper with Matthew. Cory was having a hard enough time with the idea as it was.

She pulled open the door of her car, tossed Matthew what she hoped was a careless grin and got in. As she drove away, she could see him standing in the parking lot, watching her.

As if he were still trying to figure her out.

Chapter Eight

"It's just a business meeting," Cory reminded herself, tweaking a hair into place. So why had she spent so much time fiddling with her makeup and picking out her clothes? She knew her apricot silk T-shirt brought out the golden highlights in her dark-blond hair and emphasized the brown of her eyes. She adjusted the gold buckle of her belt so it was centered on her black pants. Not exactly high fashion, but plain enough to go anywhere. She just hoped Matthew didn't show up in a suit.

Thankfully Joyce's friend had come and taken her out. Cory hadn't told Joyce that she had a date with Matthew, only that she was going out. Fortunately Joyce hadn't asked too many questions, and Cory hadn't had to use too many evasions.

She didn't want to listen to her mother's negative comments about Matthew. They often came too close to her own contradictory feelings toward him. She thought of a comment Matthew had made about the judge. It wasn't Matthew or Clifton McKnight who had made the decision. It was the judge.

And if Matthew was right about the will, then so much of her mother's struggle would be eased. She wouldn't have to work as hard. They might be able to buy their own home.

They might even have some funds to start working full-time on their catering business.

To go looking for her brothers.

As she looked at her reflection, Cory reached up and touched her chin, her cheeks, wondering once again if she looked anything like her brothers. If they shared the same eye color, if their mouths looked like hers or the shapes of their faces were the same.

What would they tell her to do about Matthew? What would their advice be?

"But they're not here," she told herself. She thought briefly of the envelope in her bedroom. She just never had time to search for them and consequently had only a pitiful amount of information and a few contacts in various government offices.

But maybe now…

She pushed herself away and without a second glance, walked out of the house.

Matthew was waiting in the lobby of the hotel when she arrived. It wasn't hard to miss his careless hair, his head bent over a magazine rack of a kiosk by the front entrance. He turned as she came in the doors, and his welcoming smile made her heart bump lightly in her chest. "Hi, there. You're nice and early," he said, coming toward her. Thankfully he wore an open-necked shirt and chinos. No suit. "You look great."

"Thank you." She couldn't think of anything wittier to say. His crooked smile, his casual grace made this seem more like a date than the business meeting Cory had convinced herself it was.

"I've got a table reserved for us. We can sit down anytime." Matthew indicated the dining room with a careful smile, and Cory followed him inside.

The Prairie Inn was the fanciest place Stratton had to offer, and it was the first time Cory had been inside. The tables in the dining room were separated by partitions of etched, smoked glass and framed with oak, creating intimacy and openness at the same time. The lighting was low, and the atmosphere inviting. As they settled into their table along one wall, Matthew looked around with an approving smile.

"Stratton is looking better all the time."

"This is a nice place," Cory agreed. "First time I've ever been here."

Matthew looked surprised. "No previous dates ever brought you here?"

"No previous dates brought me anywhere. I'm just too busy." Now didn't she sound like the town loser, Cory thought, looking quickly down.

"You and your mother do much catering?"

Cory nodded, thankful for the change in subject. "We had a couple of events last week, but that's all she can manage."

"Because of her fibromyalgia?"

Surprised that he remembered, Cory gave him another glance. "Yes. At times it's under control, but it takes a lot of time and care to keep it that way."

"Time and care that you spend on her."

"Yes." Cory held his eyes with hers. "I'm all she has right now."

"She's lucky to have you." Matthew's expression

was serious and Cory felt a moment's confusion at his sincerity.

"It's not luck. It's love," she returned quietly.

Matthew smiled slightly at that and Cory's confusion increased. This so-called business meeting was going to be harder than she thought.

The waiter came by with menus and asked if they wanted anything beforehand. Cory felt strange being served, and Matthew's covert grin told her he had noticed.

"This is hard for you, isn't it?" he said, his grin widening as he flipped open the menu. "Having someone serve you and ask you what you want."

Cory shrugged, surprised at his perception.

She gave him another quick glance over the menu, surprised to find him looking at her.

His smile was engaging, his manner casual and inviting, his charm irresistible. Though part of her instincts told her to keep her distance, she was tired of being lonely and alone. She hadn't been on a real date for years. Could barely remember which town it was in and when.

"It is difficult," she replied, smiling back. "Like you said, had we gone to the restaurant, I would have had a hard time not getting up and serving you coffee."

"Ah, yes," he said, tilting his head to one side. "I love being right."

She didn't answer, but instead studied the menu, finally deciding on a pasta dish.

"And how is your work with Mr. Stanley going?" Cory asked once the waiter left with their order.

"Good. In a couple of weeks I'll have the piles on the floor dealt with. Then we can get to work on his desk.'' He shook his head. ''How he has managed to keep clients all this time is truly amazing.''

''I guess people in small towns tend to be quite loyal. From what I hear if you need help right away, he's there for you.''

''Probably part of his problem. But I don't want to talk about Nathan Stanley. I'd sooner talk about you.''

''And here I thought this was a business meeting.'' Cory forced a light laugh to cover up the jolt his words gave her. Ordinary chatting up had been much easier.

''It is. Sort of. I do have a piece of paper I need you to sign.'' He pulled a folded-up envelope out of his shirt pocket and took out a single piece of paper, explaining to her what it meant.

Cory signed it, using the pen he handed her. He took it back, folded it back up and then put it back in his pocket. ''There. That's done. Now we can carry on.'' Matthew leaned forward again, his pose relaxed.

''That was it?''

''Yes.''

''I thought you had more to show me....'' A trill of confusion and expectation shivered down her back.

''I have to confess, it was a bit of a ruse.''

''Why?''

Matthew pulled in one corner of his lower lip, as he studied her. ''I'm not sure. A couple of things.''

''Like what?''

''Why wouldn't you dance with me at your prom?''

Cory stiffened, then forced aside her reaction. ''This is going way back,'' she said with a forced laugh.

"In a way. It was also the last time we talked to each other. And one of the only times we met outside of court."

Cory looked down, once again feeling the sting of humiliation of that evening.

"I've never had a chance to ask you why since then," Matthew continued. "I have to admit, I've always wondered. Male pride maybe," he said with a short laugh.

"There were a couple of reasons," she conceded.

"Zeke being one?"

"One part," she admitted.

"And what was the other part?"

Cory sat back, wondering what to say. How to say it. At that time in her life, Matthew had already been firmly established as the bad guy. To meet him socially had been extremely difficult for her. Especially when she had been fighting her own perfidious attraction to him for a couple of years.

"I didn't like it that you saw where my mother and I lived," she admitted. "I didn't like it that you had to see me wearing a dress that I knew was ugly. Zeke had promised to buy me a dress. But I didn't want to take anything from him." She paused a moment, to take a steadying breath, to send up another quick prayer. "So my mom went out shopping. All she could find was that pink thing. In a thrift store. We tried to fix it up as best we could. I wore it as a favor to my mom. To show her that I appreciated what she did."

In the silence that followed her comment, Cory could hear the murmuring of the other patrons of the restaurant, the faint clink of silver on china. The memory of that evening seemed to her the culmination of her and Matthew's relationship. A distinct reminder to her of the differences between them.

It had hurt more than it should.

"Yet you came. Without an escort," Matthew said, his voice gently breaking the silence.

Cory fiddled with the crease in her pants leg and smiled. "I had been asked, but I had sworn off men at that time of my life. Besides I wasn't exactly the belle of the ball, you remember." She tried to laugh it off. Tried to take refuge in her usual humor, but those very insecure years of her life could still haunt her. And Matthew was very much tied up with them. "I guess I thought you asked me as a joke."

Matthew laughed shortly. "No, Cory. Not for that reason at all." His expression became suddenly serious as he leaned forward. "You made that ordinary dress look remarkable just by wearing it, by walking around with your head up and those brown eyes daring anyone to say different."

Cory looked away, flustered. His words weren't businesslike. They had nothing to do with wills and pieces of paper. Compliments and words of admiration leaned more toward the beginnings of relationships and she didn't know how to deal with that. Not coming from Matthew McKnight.

"But I knew what you thought of me," she said quickly, as if to erase the gentle mood he had created. "I knew you didn't approve of Deirdre hanging around with me."

Matthew inclined his head. "I have to admit that was true. At first." He leaned sideways, running his thumb along his chin as he looked at her. "But that night I saw a girl who wouldn't bow to peer pressure, who didn't care what people thought of her." He was quiet a moment and Cory couldn't help but look at him. "I saw a girl that I admired."

His words rearranged and unsettled her own view of him. Never, in all her dealings with Matthew McKnight, would she have suspected admiration. Not from him.

She felt a quickening of her heart, and again she had to look away, unable to reconcile her memories and her own emotions with this new information. She had no defenses against this gentle onslaught. It was tempting to believe him totally, to accept his admiration, to think that maybe his comments, his glances, the sum total of what had been happening between them the past few days might go somewhere else. But she didn't dare.

"It couldn't have been for long. We were back in court the very next week," Cory said, bringing a strong dose of reality back into the moment.

She heard his sigh. "Yes. I know."

She sensed he was about to say more when the waiter came with their food. She welcomed the interruption, smiling her thanks at the waiter as he placed the steaming plates in front of them.

"Enjoy your food," he said, then took a step back and left them alone again.

Cory tossed Matthew a quick glance, then, folding her hands, bowed her head. Her prayers were a confusion of *Thank You and please help me* as she wondered how she was going to navigate her way through this evening.

As she raised her head, she caught Matthew's quizzical glance.

"What's wrong?" she asked, automatically touching her hair.

"Nothing. You look fine." He laughed shortly. "I find it uplifting to see how easily you express your faith."

"Praying before a meal is hardly a strong expression of faith. I've seen you pray, too."

"Yes. I guess I didn't think of you as a praying person." Silence again as he picked up his fork, toying with it. "You went to church with Zeke, but never with Joyce. Do you mind if I ask why?"

"A lawyer asking permission to ask a question?" Cory found refuge in her usual wry humor. "That's a new one."

"Can we just be Matthew and Cory tonight?" he asked. "Not a lawyer and a woman who hates lawyers?"

Cory dug her fork into her plate of pasta, wrapping the noodles around it, aware of his eyes watching her, studying her. Admit it, she thought, you like him. You've always liked him.

"Okay," she conceded with a tilt of her head.

Matthew was silent a moment. "So why church with Zeke and not Joyce?"

Cory sighed, intently watching the swirl of the noodles around her fork. She didn't want Matthew to think less of her mother and wanted him to understand. But in order for that to happen, he had to believe her view of Zeke. She wondered if he would.

"My mother had many disappointments in her life," she said, evasively.

"Her divorce from Zeke being one of them?"

Cory shook her head. "It's inevitable, isn't it? Every time we get together, there hangs the shadow of my stepfather. Can't even go out for supper, but he's there. I've spent half of my life outrunning him."

"So tell me what life with Zeke was like."

Cory took a mouthful of food, the pause giving her a chance to formulate her answer. "I don't think you'll believe me," she said finally.

Matthew sat up, his elbows on the table. "I know you well enough that you have principles and standards. I've heard Zeke's side of the story. Now I want to know yours."

"For what reason?" Why would it matter to him now?

"One of the symbols of justice is a set of scales. I've realized that in order to balance those scales, I need to hear what you have to say."

Cory played with her fork, as she tried to find the place to start, tried to find the tone that didn't sound like she was seeking sympathy, yet would tell Matthew in no uncertain terms what she and her mother lived with.

"Your mother married him when you were quite young," Matthew prompted.

"I never knew who my real father was," Cory said. "He died before I was born. My mother married Zeke when I was two. He was the only father I knew."

"And your mother divorced him when you were twelve?"

"You know your facts, Mr. McKnight," Cory said, unable to keep the sardonic tone out of her voice.

"Sorry. I'm sounding like a lawyer." Matthew leaned back. "Just ignore me. Tell your story."

Cory smiled at his admission. "Zeke Smith is, was," she corrected, "quite a charmer. My mother was overwhelmed. She was also broke with a baby girl to take care of. When Zeke proposed after only a couple of dates she accepted. She didn't know what he was really like." Cory paused, still cautious about telling Matthew, her father's one-time defender, the same things she had tried to tell many other people without success.

But Matthew said nothing, just leaned forward, his elbows resting on the table beside his untouched supper, his hands clasped loosely in front of him.

So she continued hoping she could present her mother in a positive light, aware that she wanted Matthew to see, to understand what they had to live with.

She also knew how Joyce looked to both Matthew and his father. Harsh, unyielding and sharp. They didn't know.

"Mom tried, she really did. Zeke was unpredictable in his behaviors. She never knew if he would approve or disapprove of decisions she made, things she did. One day he would tear a strip off her for spending too much on groceries, the next because she was being cheap. He would yell and throw things around and then, in a breath, would stop and apologize." She stopped, wondering if Matthew really and truly understood the tension that permeated the house living with someone like Zeke. The constant uncertainty. How could she translate that into words?

Matthew said nothing, his silence encouraging her to continue.

"I think the best examples of the real Zeke were my birthdays," she said, looking away. "I was five the first time I remember him yelling at my mother for buying me a present. It wasn't much. Just a little stuffed bear. He was going on how he wanted to be involved and how was he supposed to be a father to me if she was always taking over. So, when I was six, he took me shopping. I was allowed to pick out a doll. I was so excited. I found just the doll I wanted. Porcelain, with curly hair. But it was too expensive, he said, so I picked out another one. Same deal. Finally I found one that suited him, and I carried it to the front, happy as a clam. Then, when we got to the cashier, he pulled out his wallet. 'My goodness, no money. Sorry, honey, we'll have to do this another day.'" Cory looked Matthew straight in the eye. "The day he promised never came. When I turned eight we went through exactly the same scenario. I would get presents at Christmastime. Empty boxes. 'Full of hugs,' he would say. He was a strange man with a warped sense of humor. I stopped trusting him when I was nine."

The silence between them was absolute. Cory took a few bites of her supper, forcing them down.

"And later on…"

Cory swallowed, took a drink of water. "Lots of other promises to take me places to do things that never materialized. Always, under the surface, was this control thing. He was always ragging on my mother, calling her lazy. Among other things." Reluctantly she told him about the verbal abuse that he heaped on her mother, the humiliation, the pain her mother had to deal with as her fibromyalgia got worse and worse. "As I got older I started defending her, then I was the butt of his anger.

"Oh, he was his usual charismatic self in public. Had that aura, that charm, but at home, it was another story. At home my mother was a useless drudge, and I became someone else's kid, a waste of his money." She stopped, feeling once again the sting of humiliation, the helpless fury she felt when Zeke would start in on her mother.

"So your mother divorced him," Matthew prompted gently.

"Our home life as such was one round of fights and anger and intense pain for my mother who was told by the doctor that she was a hypochondriac. I was the one who urged my mother to leave, but she said she had made vows and promises. Zeke, however, didn't seem to think promises needed to be kept."

"Did you think he was unfaithful?"

Cory shrugged. "I don't know. Doesn't matter anymore. He didn't treat us very well. I don't imagine it would have been different with anyone else."

"So what made your mother finally decide to leave?"

Cory toyed with her fork, her appetite gone as memory after memory surfaced. "He started hitting me," she said quietly, laying down her fork, sitting back in her chair, her arms folded over her stomach.

"I recall that," Matthew said quietly. "It was in the file as an allegation."

"It was never an allegation." Cory's fingers dug into her arms remembering the questioning from social workers, psychologists and the unbelief. "It was true," she snapped. "All of it. We couldn't prove that he had been physically abusive. I was never hurt that badly. My mother took me to the doctor to get some proof, but the doctor didn't believe me or my mother. After all, he was the one who thought she was a hypochondriac."

"I'm sorry. I didn't mean that I was questioning you, Cory." Matthew sat forward, his hand resting on the table between them as if he were trying to reach out to her. "I'm just stating what was in the file."

Cory drew a slow steady breath, trying to find equilibrium. "Do you know how many years I've said what I just told you, how many times I've prayed for someone who would believe me, who would say that I was right?"

She looked up at him and was undone by the sorrow on his face. For a moment she clung to her anger, but found it hard, looking at Matthew's expression.

"It wasn't really me that he wanted, you see," Cory continued, unable to stop the flow of words now. "It was the idea that my mom had me during the week. That she had control for five days of my life. So he wanted control of the weekends. Funny thing was, I never knew if he was going to be there or not. So the times he was gone, I went home. Then he would find out, accuse my mother of encouraging me to run away, of not allowing him to have his rights...." Here Cory faltered.

"And that's where my father and I came in," Matthew finished for her.

"Yes. I guess our lawyer wasn't as convincing as you both were, because my mother always ended up losing. Trouble was, I know she didn't always come across as kind and sympathetic. Life taught her to be hard. However we still ended up with lawyers' bills. We finally paid them off a few months ago. Lawyers' fees really add up when you don't have a lot of income coming in." She glanced up at him, suddenly aware of what she was saying and the position she had put him in.

Matthew drew his hand back, frowning down at his plate. Then he picked up his fork and began eating.

They ate in silence for a while, Cory lost in her

own thoughts. She wondered what Matthew was thinking.

After a while he looked up. "You and your mother moved around a lot. Why was that?"

Cory felt the beginnings of a headache, wishing this was over. Suddenly it didn't seem as important to her as it once had.

She felt tired of Zeke and wanted him gone from their lives. For most of her life everything had revolved around him, his moods, his needs.

She didn't want to talk about Zeke anymore. For the past nine months they had lived in relative peace in Stratton. For the first time in years she and her mother could make plans for the future. God had watched over them, just as they prayed He would. What did the past matter?

"It doesn't matter, Matthew," she said quietly, taking a sip of water.

"Yes, it does," he said, glancing up. "I want to know everything. You and your mother moved around a lot. Was it to get away from Zeke?"

"Yes. We would move away, he would find us and slowly step up the intimidation. He would follow us and make threats. The stress was too much for Mom. She would get worse so we would move. I'd have to find another job and explain to each new employer why I never worked more than six months at any given job. When I first saw you in the restaurant, I thought Zeke had found us again." She felt suddenly weary. "I don't want to talk about him anymore."

Matthew pushed his plate away and sat back, his arms crossed over his chest. His mouth was curved up in a cynical smile, his eyes hard. "Can we get out of here?" he asked suddenly. "Can you stand my company a little longer? I need to go for a walk. Unless you want to finish your meal?''

"I'm not hungry," she said. "Sorry."

"Please," he said, getting up. "You of all people have the least to apologize for."

Chapter Nine

"There's a path that leads toward the river park," Cory said. "The same one you and Nathan were walking on the other Sunday. We could walk there for a while if you want."

Matthew only nodded as he held open the heavy front door of the restaurant for Cory, waiting as she stepped past him.

A heavy silence hung between them as they walked from the parking lot and toward the river. Matthew wondered how he was supposed to respond. He had pushed and prodded her to this point. She had told him what her life with Zeke Smith was like. He heard the utter sincerity in her voice, the suppressed enmity.

So how was he supposed to balance what she told him with his own experiences with the charming Zeke Smith? Was he such a fool? How could he, Matthew McKnight, who prided himself on his integrity and his innate knowledge of human beings, have been so fooled by someone?

He glanced sidelong at Cory who walked alongside

him, seemingly relaxed, thinking about what she had lived with, what she had told him.

And part of it was a result of what he and his father had done.

He wanted to believe her. Had to, if he wanted to pursue the feelings that seemed to change every time he saw her. It was the choice he had to make.

Because for better or worse, he knew every moment he spent with her, his feelings for her only grew, intensified. He didn't know why, couldn't explain it even to himself. He just knew even though she confused and frustrated him, when he was away from her, he felt lost. As if a center was gone from his life.

The path was a wide, graveled one, following the narrow river that wound through Stratton. The warmth of the day was still trapped between the trees.

"There's supposed to be some decent fishing on this river," Cory said quietly.

"I've never really gone fishing."

She only nodded and they were silent once again.

He couldn't stand it anymore, this distance between them. He didn't know what he could say to bridge the gap, to make up for all that had happened in her life.

Give me the right words, Lord, show me what to do, he prayed. He had never felt unsure around a woman before, but he did around this one.

He caught her by the arm, carefully, gently.

She stopped and turned to him, her hands clasped together, the half light of the moon casting mysterious shadows on her face.

"You're cold," he said suddenly, feeling her chilled flesh under his hand.

"Not too bad."

He could feel her faint resistance, the gentle pull she was exerting on his hand, but he didn't let her go. Instead he drew her closer.

"I want to say I'm sorry, and I don't know how to start," he said quietly. He slid his hand up her arm, to her shoulder, placed his other hand on her other shoulder. "I want to fix all that has been wrong in your life, all the things that I did, all the pain that I caused." He laughed shortly as if recognizing the enormity of what he was asking. "Cory, I don't know how else to say this except I am so very sorry for what happened, for not believing you. I'm asking you to please forgive me."

She had stopped her subtle resistance and now stood quietly in front of him. Her head was lowered, and her hands were still clasped tightly in front of her. He heard the slow intake of her breath, as if she sought control.

The moment drew out, extended and tense. Matthew wanted to urge the words out of her, anything to show that she acknowledged what he had just said. He realized in that moment that her words would change everything for him, would change everything between them.

So he waited.

Finally she looked up at him, and he was undone by the silvery line of tears down her cheeks.

"Oh, no," he whispered. "Please, don't cry." He reached up, tracing her tears, drying them. "I'm sorry. I'm so sorry."

Cory pressed her hands against her face and then he felt it. A gentle leaning toward him, a delicate acquiescence.

He slipped his arms around her, held her slender

body close, pressed her head against his shoulder. He felt a fierce desire to protect her, to try to make right what was wrong.

"Please tell me you forgive me," he whispered against her ear, her hair tangling against his mouth. "Please."

She lifted her head then, looking up at him, her eyes shimmering with the remnants of her tears.

"I've spent so much time disliking you," she said in a choked voice. "I've spent so much time fighting you, you have me all confused."

Matthew closed his eyes, resting his forehead against hers. "I wish I could make things up to you," he said quietly. "I wish I could fix what has been broken. I pray that God will forgive me as well for what happened."

He felt her gentle sigh and then her arms moved from between them, crept around him, her hands pressed lightly against his back.

Her artless response triggered something in him. Without stopping to analyze, to think, he found her mouth in a gentle kiss. But as their lips met, slowly their kiss became more intense, their arms held each other harder.

Cory pulled away, turning her head to lay it against his shoulder again. "I feel so mixed-up," she whispered, clinging to him. "I don't know what to think."

"Then don't think," he urged, running his hand up and down her back, as if coaxing her to listen. "Just let what happens, happen."

He felt her sigh, rejoiced in the pressure of her hands on his back, her arms around him.

He rocked her lightly, repeating her name, unable to believe that she was truly here, in his arms, holding him, returning his embrace. He wished that time would stop, right here, right now.

Finally she drew back, pulled her hands away, pressed them lightly against his chest. He murmured his protest, but allowed her to step back.

"I should go," she said, wrapping her arms around herself, shivering once. She looked up at him in entreaty, as if asking for his indulgence. "I have to work tomorrow."

Matthew acknowledged her words with a light nod. He had to work tomorrow, too, but it was the last thing on his mind right now.

"So what happens now, Cory?"

"It's not fair to ask that of me." She tilted her head to one side as if examining him. "This is unfamiliar territory."

He laughed shortly. "Is for me, too, Cory. I guess I was just hoping you would tell me what you want from me. What I'm allowed to give you."

She drew in a shaky breath and blinked once. "How about some space?"

That wasn't what he wanted to hear. It was a cruel echo of the same words he had used with Tricia when he broke up with her. *Space.* A euphemism for *Leave me alone.*

"How much do you need?" He tried to keep the edgy frustration out of his voice, tried to realize what she had just done. But all he could think of was the disquiet that coiled inside him at what she said. He was afraid of losing her. Now, after they had shared their first embrace, their first kiss. The kiss he had wanted to give her the night he saw her walking through a crowd of overdressed young girls in her stark simplicity and her pride.

"I don't know, Matthew. I don't know if I can shift gears this quickly." She hugged herself tighter and turned away.

He couldn't stop himself and slipped his arm across her shoulder, drawing her alongside him. "I don't want you to be confused," he said. "I just want what's best for you."

Thankfully she allowed his embrace as they walked back the way they had come. But she kept her arms close to herself this time.

When they came to the parking lot, she withdrew from him.

In silence, he walked her to her car, waiting as she unlocked it, remembering the ball practice when he said he wanted to find out who she was, when he had so casually asked her out.

He hadn't figured on what had happened to him tonight. The complete rearranging of his perceptions of Cory and, harder yet, of himself.

Just before she stepped into the car, Matthew held the door forestalling her.

"Cory," he began, uncertain of what he wanted to say, only that he didn't want her to leave without some kind of affirmation of what she felt for him. "I want to tell you, thanks."

"For what?" She stood between the door and the car, one hand on the steering wheel as if ready to jump inside.

"For trusting me with your story." He bit his lip, struggling to find the right words to say. The words that would put a smile on her face, would make her say that she cared for him. That he meant something to her. That she forgave him.

She smiled then, but it held a trace of sadness and regret. "Thanks for believing me," she replied.

"I wish…" He stopped. *Oh, Lord, the words. I need the right words.* "I wish it could have been different. From the very start."

Cory blinked and her smile faded as she understood what he meant.

Averting her eyes, she slipped into the car and tugged on the door.

Matthew closed it for her, his one hand resting on it, leaning over as he watched her start the car. He touched the window, as if trying to reach out to her.

Then she looked back over her shoulder and backed the car away.

Matthew watched her go, his emotions in a turmoil. *Go with her, Lord,* he prayed. *Let her see how I feel, what she means to me. Help her to accept it.*

Because he knew that if she didn't, his own life would never be the same.

Cory drove home, tears blurring her vision. And how was she supposed to act around Matthew now?

He had held her, had kissed her, had asked her forgiveness. No man had ever done that.

As she drove, she reached up, touching her lips with her fingers as if to relive the kiss they had shared.

It was just a kiss, she reminded herself. Just the kiss of a man who felt guilty, a way of making up for things that had gone so horribly wrong.

Yet she knew it was more than a kiss because Matthew is more than just a man. He had been her nemesis and at the same time the first man she had been attracted to. A man who created a confusion of emotions that she had never been able to reconcile. For even as Matthew had been condemning her to spending the weekends with Zeke, fighting her lawyer to assert Zeke's rights, she herself had fought her own attraction to him.

Now, with a few words, the one barrier between them was dismantled. He had admitted what he had done was wrong, had acknowledged the pain Zeke had inflicted.

I wish things could have been different. From the start. She remembered what he said about prom, how he had admired her and her tears flowed afresh. The evening she had associated with one of her greatest humiliations had suddenly been turned around, changed and renewed.

She pulled up in front of her home, laid her head on the steering wheel and closed her eyes.

I need your help, Lord. He's asked me to forgive him, told me he believes me. He's been the opponent, the enemy so long I don't know if I can do it.

Pulling in a low sigh, she got out of the car and into the now quiet house. A small light burned on the porch, and the light above the stove was lit. Cory checked on her mother, who lay fast asleep.

Relieved, she walked to her own bedroom, changed and then got into bed. She picked up her Bible, looking at it, wondering what she wanted to find.

Turning to the back, she looked up references to the word *forgive.*

With a gentle crackle of the pages, she turned to the story of Joseph. When his brothers asked for his forgiveness for what they had done, he had forgiven them. "'You intended to harm me,'" she read, "'But God intended it for good.'" Matthew hadn't really intended to harm her, had only been doing what he was hired to do. He had been as fooled by Zeke as most of the people in Riverview. Could she fault him for that?

She turned to Luke 6, starting at verse 37 and read, "'Forgive, and you will be forgiven. Give, and it will be given to you. A good measure, pressed down, shaken together and running over, will be poured into your lap. For with the measure you use, it will be measured to you.'"

How could she not forgive him? How could she say to him that what he had done was greater than many of the things she had done to others, to God? Could she stand innocent before anyone and claim that she had never done wrong, had never hurt anyone, had never caused pain and tears?

She covered her face with her hands, entreating the Lord to forgive her unforgiving heart. *As you forgave me, help me to forgive, Lord,* she prayed. *Help me to forgive.*

As she prayed it was as if a burden slowly slipped from her shoulders. She didn't have to fight what she felt for Matthew. It wasn't wrong. She wasn't betraying her mother, herself. God.

Then, following behind that, came a rush of love so profound, so pure that it almost made her laugh aloud. Free, she was finally free of anger, of hate.

Of Zeke Smith.

Thank you, Lord. Thank you.

Matthew stood by the window of his office, staring unseeing at the trees outside. He had been gone all morning to another town, sitting in on an environmental hearing for one of Nathan's clients. When he had come back, he stopped at the restaurant eager to see Cory, only to find out that she had called in to say she wasn't going to be working. He felt it would be rather presumptuous to call her so he hadn't.

He wanted to talk to her, to go over what she had told him last night.

He kept hearing Cory's voice, kept hearing what she said. Some of what she said last night wasn't new, but most of it went against all his own perceptions of Zeke. He couldn't seem to get his head around it.

He had never seen the side of Zeke Smith that Cory spoke of. Had never been on the receiving end of his anger. For him and his father, Zeke only gave the best, the most charming performance.

And was that all it was? A performance? Not the real man?

He felt betrayed and as confused as Cory said she was. He hated to think that he had been duped and recognized that his pride was as involved as his emotions.

He closed his eyes, resting his tired head against the cool glass. He hadn't slept for more than a couple of hours last night. Over and over he relived what Cory told him, what had happened between them.

The computerized beeping of the phone broke into Matthew's reverie.

He snagged the receiver, tucking it under his chin. ''Matthew McKnight here.''

''Hello, son. How are you?''

''Hi, Dad.'' Matthew dropped into his chair and pulled a pen out of its holder, catching himself glancing at the clock on the wall. A lawyer's habit. Check the time, bill the file. He put the pen down. ''What can I do for you?''

His father's heavy sigh was uncharacteristic, as was the slight pause and Matthew wondered if he was going to get one of the when-are-you-coming-home lectures his father had been doling out lately. He braced himself, ready to defend what he was doing. He liked Stratton and working with Nathan. He liked the low-key atmosphere in the office and if he were pushed, he would have to admit that right now he could stay. For an indefinite period of time.

But much of that hinged on Cory.

"An interesting turn of events just came up," Clifton said quietly. "I had a woman come into the office yesterday afternoon with what she claimed was a handwritten copy of the last will and testament of Zeke Smith."

"A holograph will?" Matthew's heart skipped a beat as his mind raced over the implications for Cory.

"Appears that way."

"Are you sure she's on the level?" Matthew asked, fiddling with the papers on his desk.

"She handed me the paper, and I checked it against other notes from Zeke I had on file," Clifton said. "Unfortunately at first glance, it appears legitimate."

Matthew shoved the file folder aside, spun his chair to glare out the window. "You're going to fight this, aren't you?" he asked, his voice clipped.

"Of course I am."

"I practically guaranteed Cory that the will was legitimate, that there would be no hindrances."

"It's okay, son. I'm not going to let this go."

Matthew shoved his hand through his hair, wondering how Cory was going to react to this particular piece of information. He knew he was falling in love with Cory. Knew that he needed her, wanted her.

He understood her bewilderment. If she found out about this new will, her precarious emotions would veer the wrong way.

He thought of Cory as a young girl clutching a doll, going to the cash register to buy it and then having her dreams dashed.

Zeke had done the same thing now. It was as if, from the grave, he had to give one final twist to the knife.

And as Matthew analyzed this thought, he realized that any doubts he might have had over what Cory had said about Zeke, were once and for all dissipated.

"Even if we fight it, the proceeds will have to come out of the estate," Matthew said heavily.

"I know. I'm going to try to expedite this as quickly as possible."

"What's the date on it?"

"A year ago. The will I filed is, unfortunately, four years old."

"How come we never heard of her before?"

"That's one of my arguments, however I haven't been in contact with Zeke a couple of years now. Anything could have happened in that time."

Matthew pinched the bridge of his nose. He could feel a headache coming on. And a heartache. How was he going to tell Cory?

Why tell her at all? The thought was tantalizing. However, if this woman's claim was legitimate, sooner or later it would come out. For now, though, he opted for later.

"Matthew, are you okay?"

"Yeah," Matthew answered. "I'm okay. Keep me posted. And if there's anything I can do on this end, let me know."

"Well, you'll have to keep Cory apprised of what is happening."

He knew he had to. But not yet. Not while their relationship, if he could be so presumptuous to call it that, was so new and fragile. Matthew had been the one to encourage her to take the estate and now things were transpiring almost exactly as she said they would.

"Thanks, Dad. I'll be praying for a positive result." Matthew said goodbye and reaching around, dropped the phone in the cradle. He dropped his head back and dragged his hands over his face. *Oh, Lord. We could have done without this particular mess,* he prayed. *How am I going to deal with this?*

He turned back to the desk, wondering how he was going to concentrate on his work for the rest of the day. It was only three o'clock. In a couple of hours he had to head to ball practice.

And Cory.

His heart quickened at the thought and he knew that for now, he wasn't going to tell her about the will. He was going to wait and see what feat of lawyering his dad could pull off to head off this particular disaster.

There was no way they could have foreseen another will, but he was sure she was going to once again feel the sting of betrayal.

And he was the one who put her in that position. Had made her, once again, vulnerable to Zeke Smith.

A wave of inexpressible anger flowed through him. He thought of Cory, at the mercy of this man. How could he and his father have been so wrong?

A slight knock at the door made him look up. It was Nathan.

"Can I come in?" he asked.

"Of course," Matthew said, getting up and pulling a chair out for him. "This is your place, after all."

Nathan shrugged as he sat down in the chair. "My building. Your office." He leaned back, folding his hands over his stomach. "You've been here a few weeks now. I just thought I'd see how things are going."

Matthew smiled, glad for the momentary reprieve from his circling thoughts. "They're going well. I like the work. There's more variety than I thought there would be in a small town."

"Well we have our marital intrigues and wheelers and dealers just like any big place like Riverview," Nathan said with a grin. "By the way, I got a compliment from Dick and Edna Thachuk on the incorporation you handled for their company. They are quite pleased with some of the advice you gave them. I have to confess I wouldn't have thought of it."

"It wasn't difficult. Something I had done for another client in Riverview," Matthew said casually, shrugging the compliment away, even though it made him feel good. Too often in his work in Riverview it was complaints he heard. Never, to his knowledge, compliments.

"You seem a lot more relaxed than you were when you first came," Nathan added. "I think this town agrees with you."

"I like it here," he agreed, toying with his pen. "I like the pace of the work."

"And the restaurant is just across the road. Very convenient for a bachelor. And that Cory is such a fun waitress."

Matthew hoped his expression hadn't changed, but

he couldn't seem to stop the silly quickening of his heart at her name. He didn't reply.

"That's fine," Nathan said with a grin. "Try to keep your secrets. Hard to do in a town this size. I understand you went out for supper last night with her."

"Really?"

"Yes. At the Prairie Inn."

Matthew shook his head, unable to stop the smile that teased his mouth. "And what did we order?"

"Oh, come now. Even in Stratton we recognize that some things are private." Nathan smiled again. "Actually I had to deliver a message to you from Cory. Said something about not being able to come to practice tonight."

"Did she say why?"

"Nope. Just wouldn't be able to come."

Matthew acknowledged the information, chewing his lip. Was she trying to avoid him? Had he pushed things too hard last night? "Thanks, Nathan," he said, distracted by his thoughts.

"If you want to know, I'm sure she wouldn't mind if you stopped by her house later on." Nathan smirked, a man totally in the know.

Matthew laughed lightly. "I don't even know where she lives."

"West of Main Street, across from the feed mill."

"How do you know?"

"No secrets in Stratton. Remember?" Nathan stood up and stretched. "Well, I'm done for the day. Don't stay too long." He held Matthew's gaze. "And check up on Cory. She might be sick, you know."

"Thanks for the tip."

"I'll send you the bill." Nathan closed the door behind himself.

Matthew grabbed the file he had so angrily shoved away, flipped a few pages and picked up his pen to finish up. But he couldn't concentrate. He wondered if Cory was sick, as Nathan had intimated.

He thought of the kiss they had shared. How she had drifted into his embrace.

Once again he prayed. Once again he asked the Lord for wisdom, for patience. He asked for good things for Cory, who'd had to deal with so much in her young life.

He felt a surge of protectiveness, a desire to surround her with only good things.

With love.

Chapter Ten

Cory dropped onto the couch and swung her feet up. She felt drained and exhausted, but at least her mother was sleeping peacefully for now.

She glanced at the clock. Only five-thirty. She should get up and make something to eat but it seemed pointless for just one person.

For now all she wanted to do was sleep. She had laundry to fold and a few shirts to iron, but she was too tired.

Just a few moments, she promised herself, curling up. Then she could get at the rest of the work.

She closed her eyes, but when she did she saw the same thing, felt the same thing she had all day.

Matthew's head bending toward her, his soft lips touching hers.

She hugged herself, a feeling of yearning shivering through her. Last night she had come to a turning point, a realization that her feelings for Matthew were real, true and, above all, allowed. She had looked forward with a child's anticipation to the day, to seeing Matthew in the restaurant.

This morning it had been almost agonizing to find out that her mother had the flu. That she needed Cory to stay home.

She closed her eyes, easily summoning Matthew's features, his face. Then, with the memory of his sea-green eyes holding hers, she slowly drifted away from the reality of a sick mother and the tangle of her own bemused thoughts into a place full of warmth, security and love.

Matthew's arms.

"Cory? Cory? Hello?"

Woven through the dream was the sound of his voice. Concerned, curious.

The voice grew louder, interspersed with the sound of knocking. She struggled to separate it from her dreams. Was someone here? She heard the sound of a door close in the front hallway and she fought to open her eyes, to wake up.

Slowly she sat up, looking around at the room suffused with early evening light. Had she been dreaming? Was she still?

"Cory, can I come in?"

Her heart tripped, then started up again, faster than before as she realized she was wide-awake and she recognized the voice.

It was Matthew, and he was in her home.

She ran her hands over her unruly hair, loosened from its ponytail, straightened her T-shirt, tucking it back into her faded blue jeans, then got up.

"Come in," she said, clearing a throat still thick with sleep. As she spoke, she saw a shadow move in the front hall. Then Matthew stood in the doorway of the living room. He wore the same baggy T-shirt he had the first time they had coached together, the same faded and worn blue jeans. His hair was wind-tossed, and his eyes were concerned.

"Hi, there," he said softly. "I missed you at ball practice."

Cory fought to pull herself together, to think coherently. "I left a message with Nathan. Didn't he tell you?"

"He did." Matthew's eyes held hers. "You weren't at the restaurant, either."

Her heart gave a little jump at the thought that he had gone looking for her, had missed her.

"My mom has the flu so I had to stay home to help her." She couldn't stop herself from running her fingers through her hair in a feeble attempt to straighten it. She felt unkempt and unready to meet him.

"And you're okay?" Matthew asked, his eyes searching her face, as if looking for evidence.

"I'm just tired."

His smile sent a shiver of warmth through her as he took a step nearer. "Did you have supper?"

She shook her head. "No. I've been too busy." Why was she talking about such prosaic things when the man who had lingered in her dreams, who had taken up so much of her emotions the past few days was standing in her home?

"Do you want me to make you something?" he asked.

"No, no. That's okay. I'm really not hungry." She didn't want him going through their kitchen. Bad enough that he was in their house, had seen where and how they lived. She couldn't help but glance behind her at the couch she had just lain on. It looked as if it still held the imprint of her body, it sagged so badly. "I can make you a cup of tea or coffee, though," she said, turning her attention back to him.

"Tea sounds good. I drank too much coffee already." He slipped his hands into the back pockets of his blue jeans, rocking back on the heels of his running shoes. "You sure you don't want any help? I do know how to boil water."

"I'm sure." She retreated to the kitchen, put the kettle on, pulled out a package of cookies, keeping herself busy in there while she sensed him wandering around the living room. She tried not to let herself see their home through his eyes. It was plain, worn and veering on shabby.

Please, Lord, she prayed, *I don't want to be ashamed. I know it shouldn't matter. It means so much to me that he thinks well of me.*

The water boiled. She made tea and brought it out on a tray with her best mugs. Then, taking a deep breath, sending up another prayer for courage, she walked into the living room.

Matthew turned as she entered the small room. He was looking at a group of her school pictures.

"Quite a metamorphosis," he said with a teasing grin.

Cory groaned as she set the tray down on the low coffee table. "Mom insisted on not only buying my school picture every year, she also hangs them up everywhere we go."

She set out the cups, the sugar and the plate then glanced up at him, discomfited to find him looking at her, his expression suddenly serious.

"How often did you and your mother move around?"

Cory held the tray in front of her, like a shield. She heard a tone of sorrow in his voice, suffused with regret. "It doesn't matter anymore, Matthew," she said quietly. "I want you to know that."

"Please tell me."

Cory bit her lip and then slowly shook her head. "That's all in the past. Zeke Smith doesn't have a hold over me or my mother anymore." She laughed lightly. "And now, thanks to his will, I can afford to make a few plans." She smiled brightly at him, wondering why he wasn't smiling back. "So, it doesn't matter how often, or where," she continued. "I will tell you, though, that we've been through a lot of furniture."

She wanted to say that. To let him know that their present situation didn't result from poor money management, but extenuating circumstances.

"What do you mean?"

"Just that every time we moved, we were in a bit of a hurry and often left the big stuff behind." She shrugged lightly, as if to dismiss it. "Too hard to pack into a station wagon."

"Cory…"

She held up her hand. "Don't. Please." She gestured to the couch. "Now, come and drink some tea and have some delicious cookies, which I bought all by myself."

He smiled a slow, wistful smile. "You are really someone special, Cory," he said, his voice quiet.

"I'm afraid you'll find that I'm frighteningly ordinary," she said. "Now, let's have a cup of tea."

He conceded the end of that particular conversation and sat on the couch beside her. He leaned back and then sat up again.

"What's this?" He pulled out an old, worn photo album that had been lying on the couch, then set his mug down. "Pictures. Of you?" he asked with a slow grin.

"No. Not really." She tried to laugh, but couldn't. It seemed the entire history of her life would be shown to this man one way or the other. "I found that when I was in tenth grade. I didn't even know Mom had it up until then. It's of my brothers." She took her mug and tucking her legs up under her, curled up in her corner of the couch.

"Brothers?" Matthew frowned as he carefully opened the hard brown cover. "I didn't know you had brothers."

"It wasn't something Mom wanted to be common knowledge. She hadn't even told Zeke." Cory held her mug tightly between both hands, her elbows pressed against her sides. What would he think of her mother now?

Matthew was silent as he turned pages, the protective paper rustling. Cory just about knew the album by heart, the faded color pictures, cracked with age, but carefully pasted on the pages. He turned back to the first page.

"That's my mother and my real father," Cory said as he glanced up at her questioningly. "Andrew Luciuk. He died when my mother was about two months pregnant with me. He's the father of my brothers as well, in case you're wondering."

Matthew turned the page to the meager collection of pictures of two boys. "And these boys. What happened to them?"

Cory swallowed down a knot of pain. Why did it bother her now? Why should it? Was it because she knew of Matthew's very intact and very secure family? Was it because it mattered so much to her what he thought of her, of her mother?

She took a careful sip of tea and prayed a quick prayer. "You are going to be really sick and tired of the brief history of Cory Luciuk by tonight," she said with a light attempt at dispelling the growing heavy atmosphere.

"I doubt that," he replied. "Tell me."

And once again, Cory was bringing out details of her life that she and her mother had kept to themselves. "My mom was expecting me when my father died. My father had no life insurance and hadn't worked for about half a year, and my mother had never really worked. The boys were very young. Mom had absolutely no money so she and the boys were evicted from their apartment. She had no family to help her out. Things were pretty dismal. Then she found out she was expecting me. She went to Social Services to see what they could do. A social worker encouraged her to put the boys up for adoption. It was an extreme measure, but by that time she had already been unsuccessfully looking for work for about four months. She had lived in a shelter the whole time. She didn't know where to turn. So she gave them up. She did it out of love for the boys." Cory paused, feeling anew her mother's pain at that irrevocable decision. "She wasn't told where they went or what happened to them. Open adoptions weren't encouraged at that time. She was easily intimidated then and when the social worker told her that it would be better if she stayed out of the boys' lives, that's what she did. I don't know how she managed to get through the next year. She never talks about it.

She even contemplated giving me up to give me a chance at a better life. But I guess things turned around for her, because she got a job, a place to stay and then she met Zeke Smith.''

"And you don't know anything about your brothers?''

Cory stared down at the brown liquid in her mug, swirling it around. ''I know their first names and dates of birth, but that's it.'' She couldn't look up at him. ''I didn't know where to start looking. How to find them. I tried off and on, but it's so hard to get any information. I never stuck with it long enough to find anyone in any department willing to help.''

Matthew said nothing, only looked a little more closely at the pictures then angled the album toward Cory. ''Cute kids. What are their names?''

Cory put her mug down and moved a little closer. ''This one with the dark hair and the serious look is Jake. This other one with the mischievous grin is Simon.'' She touched the pictures gently, as if trying to breathe life into the figures she had only known as pictures. ''When I first saw the pictures I used to pretend that one day they would come charging into my life to save me and my mom....'' she paused, realizing who she had prayed for these brothers to rescue her from. Zeke. Clifton. Matthew.

"And they never came, I gather,'' Matthew said quietly, turning to face her.

She laughed lightly. ''No. They never did.''

Matthew set the album down, his elbows resting on his knees. ''And you don't know anything more?''

"No.''

Matthew angled his head toward her, his chin resting on his shoulder, his eyes holding hers. ''And what about now, Cory? Do you still wish they would come into your life and rescue you?''

Cory felt the full impact of his gaze, heard the import of his question. She looked quickly down at her now cold tea and shook her head. "No. I don't think so."

Matthew turned to her, gently took the cup from her hands. He drew in a slow breath as he toyed with her fingers. "Last night you told me you wanted space, time. I know that twenty-four hours is hardly enough." He squeezed her hands, his eyes intent on hers. "I've been thinking about you. About me. About our complex history. And about what I'd meant when I told you that I wished things had been different from the start." He lifted her hand and brushed his lips across it.

Cory swallowed at the sight of his head bent over her hands, the touch of his lips on them. "At the prom?" she asked, licking her lips nervously.

"No. Before that." He looked up at her, a sad smile hovering over his lips. "I was waiting for my dad at the courthouse. When I saw you I didn't know who you were, even how old you were, but I couldn't avoid the pull of attraction you had. You seemed so old, so mature. So poised."

"That was a long time ago," she said quietly.

"I didn't find out how old you were until my dad told me. I felt like a reprobate, but I couldn't seem to keep my eyes off you."

Cory smiled at his confession. "How old were you then?"

"About twenty-two." He smiled ruefully. "I was articling for my father that year. Student lawyer and a know-it-all, and I fell for a teenage girl with sharp eyes and a sharp tongue.''

Cory couldn't stop the flush that warmed her neck. "I used to have some pretty smart remarks, I'll admit.''

"I remember one comment you threw out at me. It was pretty funny. Even then,'' he continued.

"Please,'' she begged. "Like you said, I was young. I didn't have a lot of defenses. Mouthing off was all I could do.''

But he kept on. "You came out of the courtroom, stopped right in front of me and said, 'If it wasn't for lawyers we wouldn't need them,' then turned around and marched away. My dad was dumbfounded, Zeke was furious and I had to bite my lip from laughing. Once I got it, mind you.'' He stopped, his hands caressing hers. He took a slow breath, as if for courage and Cory looked up at him, tension coiling in her stomach at the somber tone of his voice.

He sighed, reached out and lightly touched her cheek. "I'd like to see more of you.''

Cory felt each word press down on her mind, permeating her very being, slowly pushing away her flimsy defenses. She closed her eyes, as if to hear them better, as if to hold them closer.

His fingers lingered on her face, tracing her features as she sat stock-still, light shivers dancing up and down her spine at his gentle caress.

She turned her face toward his hand, reaching up to hold it against her cheek, a peculiar sorrow mixed with serenity.

"I know you wanted space,'' he continued, his voice quiet, intimate. "I'm not really giving you that, am I?''

Cory pulled away, still holding his hand. "Last night was..." She shook her head, reaching, struggling to find the right words. "It was difficult and yet not." She turned his hand over, lightly tracing the lines in his palm. "I was overwhelmed and didn't quite know what to think and how to sort everything out. I've always liked things set out in black and white. From the start you've been a grey area to me."

"What do you mean?" His voice was soft, hesitant.

She looked up at him, his hand pressed between hers. "I remember hating what you did, and then looking at you and wishing that someday you would smile at me. There were times I honestly thought I was crazy. Like I was betraying my mom, betraying myself." She laughed lightly. "I think I've always liked you. At the prom, after I told you to get lost, I was kicking myself afterward for being such a snob. I was scared of you. Scared of what you would think of a poor girl who couldn't even afford a decent dress, who lived in a run-down apartment block in the wrong part of town. I didn't want it to matter and I hated that it did. You've been the enemy and yet..." she couldn't finish, still unable to articulate her own confusion.

Matthew smiled at her then. A warm, welcoming smile that promised much more. He lay back against the couch and tugged on Cory's hands. "I hope I'm not the enemy anymore?" he said, a gentle question in his voice.

"It depends on what I'm fighting," she replied.

"Don't fight." Then he lowered his head, his lips touched hers and once again he drew her close into a place of warmth, strength and sanctuary.

She shifted and slipped her arms around him, exulting in the strength of his arms around her, savoring the feel of Matthew holding her tight.

"Oh, Cory," he murmured in her ear. "You don't know how badly I wanted to do this from the first moment I stepped into the house. When I didn't see you at the restaurant this morning I felt lost." He pulled back, tilting her chin up to look at him. "I missed you and I was scared."

"You? Scared?" The thought seemed ludicrous. "Of what?"

"Scared that you might run away again."

Cory laid her head against the back of the couch, her eyes on this handsome man who wanted to be with her, who felt lost when she wasn't around. It was a small miracle, she reflected.

"I don't have any place I'd sooner be right now," she said quietly.

"I'm glad," he said.

"There's something else I need to tell you. About last night…when you asked my forgiveness…" She held his steady gaze, feeling a tension in the hands that lay on her shoulders. "I have to admit that there had been many times that I thought I hated you. But like I said, you were always a grey area. More than anything I hated the feeling that no one was listening to me. That I was helpless, that I had no rights."

Matthew made a murmur of regret and she touched his mouth, forestalling the words.

"I don't know how to say this without sounding all formal, but yes, I forgive you. I need forgiveness as much as anyone. If I think of all the trouble I must have caused you and your father..." she paused, then laughed lightly, "It doesn't matter now, does it?"

"What matters is that you've forgiven me," Matthew said, cupping her face in his hand. "And I thank God for that."

Chapter Eleven

Matthew held Cory close, her head tucked under his chin. He felt complete. Whole. His chest lifted in a satisfied sigh as he silently sent up a prayer of thanks.

"I have a confession to make," he said quietly, staring at her school pictures hanging on the wall across from him. "I came to Stratton for more than one reason, although I don't think I wanted to admit it at the time. I was looking forward to seeing you even though I knew you wouldn't welcome me."

Cory laughed lightly, acknowledging the truth of the statement. "When I first saw you in the restaurant, I was scared stiff that Zeke was going to be coming as well. And then I was mad."

"I gathered that." Matthew smiled in remembrance.

"When you first wanted me to sign that will, to accept the money from Zeke, I thought it would make things too easy for you. I thought it would salve your conscience, and I didn't want that to happen." She pulled back then, looking him straight in the eye. "I didn't want anything good to come out of his death. But it did. Money isn't that important to me, or my mother. But we've done without so long, because of Zeke, it almost seems a type of divine justice that something should come back. Doesn't it?''

Fear clawed up his throat as he held her trusting gaze. He couldn't tell her. Not yet. What they shared was so fragile. If he told her what his father had related to him just this afternoon, she would be angry again. He couldn't face that.

Instead he bent his head and kissed her, closing his eyes against the open trust he saw in hers, closing his mind to what might happen, praying his father would work a miracle for them.

Cory pulled slowly away, pressing her hand on his chest, looking guilty. She lifted her hands to smooth down her hair, slanting a furtive glance at Matthew.

"My mother," she said quietly, getting up. "I should check on her."

The moment was broken with the mention of Joyce. Matthew wondered what Joyce would have to say if she found out that he was in the house. He doubted much had changed since she had turned away from him in church.

Cory walked out of the living room, and Matthew watched her go with a small measure of fear.

"She is so great," he whispered clutching his head. "I can't tell her. I just can't."

He shut his eyes against the flare of shame when he thought of deceiving her. *Please, Lord, just give me some more time with her without that. Just let me show her how much I care for her.* He didn't know if his prayer was legitimate, but he knew that right now he needed help through this situation.

All he needed was a little more time to cement the relationship. Once he had established that, only then might she be able to accept what he had to tell her.

He needed time to prove himself trustworthy, he thought, getting up.

As he did, the photo album he had been looking at fell to the ground. He picked it up and opened it again. Then, as he looked at the pictures of the brothers Cory used to wish for, he knew what he could do.

He and his father had enough connections in the legal world. Someone, somewhere would know of these men.

Jake and Simon. Matthew carefully pulled a picture of the two of them out of the book and slipped it into his pocket. Then he put the photo album back on the shelf with the few others Cory and her mother had.

He fingered one of the others; then, with a pensive smile, pulled it out and opened it up.

A young Cory grinned back at him. A gap-toothed smile. The caption told him that she was seven years old and had just lost her front teeth.

He paged through the album noting that there were very few pictures of Joyce. He wondered if she was the one who took most of the pictures.

"You're not allowed to do that yet," Cory said from the hallway.

Matthew turned, feeling guilty until he saw her grin. "It's called research," he said easily. "I always do that before I start on a new case."

"Oh. So that's what I am?"

"Of course. I'll just have to put off my other clients so I can give you my full attention." He returned her smile, enjoying the bantering. It injected a light note into what, up until now, had been deeply intense.

"Nathan won't be pleased if you neglect your work."

"That's okay," he said with a grin. "I'm just working there until a good fast-food job opens up."

"I think your reality check just bounced," Cory returned. "You'd be hopeless in the kitchen."

"I resent that."

"Good. You can prove me wrong." She threw him a teasing look over her shoulder. "I'm going to make some supper for my mother. You can help."

"Is she awake?"

"No. But she's slept long enough. She should eat something." Cory bit her lip, glancing sidelong at him.

"And what is she going to say when she finds me here?"

Cory lifted her shoulder in a shrug. "I guess I'll have to handle that as it comes up."

Matthew held her gaze. "I'll be here, Cory."

"I know. Now, lets get that kitchen tidied up," she said, turning away. "I feel like I should apologize for the mess, but this week has felt like every day was Monday."

"That's rough," he sympathized. "Well, point me in the direction of the soap, and I'll wash these dishes."

"Under the sink," she pointed with her chin as she opened the fridge. "I was kidding, but I'm also not going to turn down the help."

Matthew glanced over his shoulder. "I don't think any man was ever punished for doing the dishes."

"Not in this house." Cory kicked the door of the fridge closed with her foot.

"What are you making?"

Cory grinned and held up an egg. "Nature's fast food. I'm making an omelette. You want one?"

"Are you going to put onions in it?"

"Don't tell me you're fussy?"

"Well—" Matthew threw her an apologetic look "—I'm not a big fan of onions."

Cory shook her head, winking at him. "I never would have figured you for a picky eater."

He smiled back at her, their eyes holding, lengthening the moment. Then she turned back to her omelette and he went back to washing dishes, working together in companionable silence.

Matthew couldn't help but wonder what it would be like to have Cory around all the time. To share a life together.

Hold on, Matthew, he warned himself. He was jumping way too far ahead. Last night he had kissed her for the first time. He had never moved this quickly with any of the other women he had dated.

You've never known any of the other women as long as you've known Cory, he reminded himself.

"You're sure quiet all of a sudden," Cory said, brushing past him to pull a frying pan out of the oven.

He set the last cup on the drain board and turned to her. "Just lost in thought, I guess."

"Unfamiliar territory?" She set the pan on the stove and threw him a saucy grin.

"Nasty, nasty," he reprimanded. He caught her hand and tugged, pulling her closer.

"I have to cook this omelette," she said, putting up a token resistance.

"I know." He dropped a quick kiss on her mouth, just because he knew he could. It was as if he couldn't hold her enough, couldn't touch her enough.

The sound of a door opening down the hallway made her pull away with a guilty start. Cory threw a furtive glance down the hallway and moved away from Matthew.

"Hi, Mom. I was just going to get you," she said to Joyce.

Joyce glanced from Matthew to Cory, who now stood in front of her, fidgeting.

"Hi, sweetheart," Joyce said to Cory. She turned to Matthew. "And hello, Mr. McKnight. I didn't know you were here."

"How are you feeling, Mom?" Cory put an arm carefully around her shoulders. "Do you want to sit in the living room?"

"I'm okay, Cory. I'll sit by the table. If I'm not going to be in the way, that is?" She looked at Matthew with an appraising look. It wasn't difficult to ascertain that in spite of her daughter's changed heart, Joyce still didn't trust him.

Cory settled her mother in and went back to the stove. She didn't look at Matthew when she turned the heat on under the frying pan. She pulled open the utensil drawer and fumbled around for a fork which she immediately dropped. When she bent over to pick it up, she banged her head on the oven door handle.

"Excuse me," she muttered, throwing the fork into the sink and grabbing another one.

Matthew watched her awkward movements. She was nervous. A nervousness created by her mother's presence and Joyce's unspoken censure of Matthew, no doubt.

He figured it would be better if he left Cory to work alone and walked around the U-shaped kitchen and sat down at the table across from Joyce. He preferred to face her head-on. She looked at him, her arms crossed over her chest.

"So what brings you here, Mr. McKnight. More business about the will?"

Matthew felt his pulse quicken at her question, wondering for a guilty moment if she knew.

"Actually, I just came to see how Cory was doing," he said smoothly. "She was supposed to help me coach T-ball this afternoon, and she couldn't make it." He looked up at Joyce then, forcing himself to hold her piercing gaze. "I was concerned."

"I find this interesting," Joyce said quietly. "You didn't seem so concerned about her before. When Zeke was on the rampage."

Matthew acknowledged her comment with a slight nod. "No. My concern had been for my client. Misplaced concern, I found out."

"Found out? Or decided to set aside now that Cory is older, prettier? Now that some time has elapsed." Joyce rocked back and forth with slow movements, her eyes never leaving Matthew. "I know how you used to look at her, Matthew, watch her when you thought no one could see you. But I did. I know you were attracted to her."

"Mother, please," Cory stepped around the cupboards. "I don't want you talking to Matthew like this."

But Joyce didn't move her eyes from Matthew once.

"You're right, Joyce," Matthew conceded. "I've always been attracted to her. Cory is a very dynamic person. Hard to look past."

He could see his honest admission took a little of

the wind out of her sails and for a moment Joyce stopped her rocking.

"And I've since found out a few things about my former client, Zeke Smith." He felt as if he had come to a crucial point and he wanted and needed this tiny woman's approval. "Things that, I must confess, I've been blind to."

"Convenient, isn't it, to discover that after the man is dead?"

"Actually, it isn't." Matthew sat back and sighed lightly. *Please, Lord, give me the right words. Let her see that I'm sincere.* It meant everything to him to know that this woman believed him. This woman whose hatred for him was even stronger than Cory's had been. "Last night I asked Cory's forgiveness for the trouble and pain I caused by defending Zeke Smith's rights. I could hide behind the excuse that I was protecting his court-ordered rights. Doing my job. I know now how manipulative Zeke was. I could argue that I fell under his spell as well." He straightened, still holding Joyce's gimlet gaze. "But none of that really matters now. Right now, I only ask that you can forgive me for the trouble I inadvertently brought into your life."

Joyce held his gaze, then looked away, as if to another time. "Did you know that whenever Cory had to visit him, I would be sick with worry?" Her voice was quiet but determined. "Sick with wondering what would happen to her, what he would do to her. I used to pray, but I stopped doing even that." She stopped, pressing a hand to her mouth.

Cory was instantly at her side, her arm around her shoulders, her hand covering her mother's. "Don't, Mom. Don't go there. It's over now."

"It's only been over for us for a few weeks, Cory," Joyce said angrily. "Up until this man came, we thought Zeke would show up any moment and we would have to move again." Her voice faltered. "And he comes telling us that Zeke has given us everything he owns. I don't believe it."

Her words cut through Matthew and for a moment he wanted to tell them that they were both right not to trust.

Then Cory looked at him, her eyes shining with affection and, maybe, love? He couldn't extinguish that. Not while everything was so new between them.

"But it's true," Cory said confidently, "It's real. I saw the will. And now we can make some plans." She turned back to her mother, and Matthew felt almost sick.

"Plans. We've never been able to make plans." Joyce covered her face with her hands, and Matthew could see the sheen of tears slipping between her fingers. He felt helpless and out of place. He felt like a deceiver.

Cory gave him a helpless look, still crouched by her mother's side.

It was all he could do to keep from rushing to her side, from pulling her away from her mother, from gathering her in his arms. He wanted to protect her from the truth. To keep it at bay until they had a chance to spend some time together without the specter of Zeke and his manipulation hanging between them.

He felt as if he balanced on a very tricky edge. Faced with Joyce's real pain, the knowledge of Zeke's latest will seared his mind. Zeke was everything Joyce and Cory had always said he was. In spite of his fine words to Joyce, Matthew knew that he hadn't believed Cory until he experienced for himself the very nature of Zeke Smith. They were both right. Had been right all along.

"I want him to leave, Cory," Joyce said quietly.

"No, Mom," Cory said, stroking her mother's hair. "I asked him to stay for supper."

Joyce lifted her face, palming away the tears, staring at Cory. "He was your date last night, wasn't he?"

Matthew listened to the mother and daughter, a slow pain building in his chest at what he heard. Cory hadn't told her mother she had been with him.

"Yes, he was," Cory said quietly.

"Why didn't you tell me?"

"I knew it would upset you."

"I would have stopped you."

"You wouldn't have, Mother. I would have gone anyhow." Cory looked over at Matthew, her smile reassuring. "I wanted to see him," she said, her eyes holding his. "I wanted to be with him. You see, I've liked him for years."

Her quiet admission eased his pain. When she got up to stand beside him, he couldn't stop himself from catching her hand, squeezing it tightly.

Joyce sat in stony silence not looking at either of them. Matthew thought of the last time he saw her in church. At that time both Cory and her mother treated him the same. Now Joyce sat alone in her anger, and Cory stood trustingly by his side.

"He's not to be trusted, Cory," Joyce said quietly.

"Why do you say that? You don't know him."

Joyce looked up at her, shaking her head. "And you don't either, my girl. Before last night you felt the same way I did. Don't be a fool like me and fall for a charming smile and a handsome face." And with those words hanging in the air, Joyce got carefully up and walked back to her bedroom.

Cory watched her go, and Matthew could see the pain in her face. He felt her gently tug on his hand. For a moment he wanted to hang on, to keep her at his side, to keep her away from the bitter anger of her mother and the truth.

But he let her go.

"I'll be right back," Cory said, walking backwards down the hall. "Don't go."

Matthew shoved his hands in his pockets, smiling sadly as she turned and entered her mother's bedroom.

He smelled something and ran to the stove. He turned the heat off under the pan, pulled it off the element and stared with consternation at the burnt omelette.

"So much for supper," he muttered, dropping the smoking pan into the sink. He cleaned it up as best he could, then put the pan back on the stove.

"I'm sorry," Cory said behind him. "I forgot about it."

Matthew turned, leaning back against the counter. "I wasn't hungry, anyway."

Cory walked toward Matthew and reaching up, pressed her fingers against his forehead. "Stop frowning, Matthew. Everything will be fine."

"Can I see you again?" he asked, almost desperately.

Cory's smile lit up her face, reassuring him. "Of course."

"I have to sit in on a meeting for Nathan on Saturday. But can I pick you up on Sunday? For church?"

"That would be nice."

"Good." He shifted his weight, feeling suddenly awkward. "I'll see you then." He laid his hands on her shoulders, drew her close and kissed her once more.

Just one more time together, he thought, holding her close. Then I'll tell her. Sometime next week, I'll tell her.

"You look particularly ravishing for a Saturday morning," Kelsey said as Cory laid an order on the counter for the cooks.

Cory glanced down at her apron already stained with tomato sauce, her shirt wrinkled and damp at the back. "Oh, very ravishing," she said with a sardonic smile. "I'm expecting a photographer for *Today's Christian Woman* for an exclusive interview."

Kelsey propped herself against the counter, pursing her lips as she looked her friend over. "Of course you are. And she or he is going to do an article on, 'What the Woman in Love Looks Like.'"

Cory tried to frown, but couldn't. It was as if her face refused to cooperate. "Well, I certainly don't look ravishing," she said.

"Wow. Snappy comeback, Cory. You're definitely twitter-pated, my girl." Kelsey just grinned.

"I'm not. I'm busy is what I am."

"And is the very charming and handsome Mr. McKnight coming into the restaurant today?"

Cory turned to her friend, shaking her head. "No. He's gone to a meeting for Nathan in another town."

"Oh. So we know his comings and goings do we?"

Kelsey caught her friend by the arm and pulled her into a narrow hallway, away from the kitchen and the dining area, her eyes shining with anticipation. "I heard you guys were together in the Prairie Inn the other night." Kelsey waved an admonishing finger. "Patronizing the competition, are we?"

"Matthew asked me out." Cory stopped herself. "No. He had to talk to me about the will." Cory couldn't stop the flush from creeping up her neck as she remembered that night and then yesterday. Matthew's gentle touch, his concern, his expression of love.

"So, are you in love?"

"Kelsey, stop it," Cory reprimanded, the flush warming her cheeks now.

"Guilty as charged," crowed Kelsey, squeezing her friend's arm. "You do love him, don't you?"

Cory felt it again. The faint hesitation. "I care for him," she said carefully, avoiding Kelsey's avid gaze. "He's really nice...."

"Oh, no," Kelsey wailed. "I hear that 'but' in your voice. Why are you doing this to yourself?"

Cory bit her lip, shaking her head. "I've never felt this way about any guy before." Now she looked at Kelsey, bewildered. "And I'm scared."

"Of what? He's good-looking, he's got all his teeth, he's got a good job. He goes to church. Honey, it doesn't get much better."

How could Cory explain it to Kelsey who had grown up with security—parents who were still together, who lived in the same town they were born in? Kelsey's previous husband had been a wonderful man, according to Kelsey. "I guess I keep thinking about Zeke," she said quietly. "He's been the only significant male in my life, and you know how horrible that was." Cory stopped, knowing Kelsey wouldn't truly understand. "My mother keeps telling me to be careful. Not to trust him."

"Do you?"

Cory stopped. "I don't know," she said softly. "I trust him to tell the truth, to take care of me."

"So what's left?"

"What if he changes, Kelsey? What if he is just like my stepfather? Lately Mom has been pining over my brothers, and I think how much you open yourself up to pain when you care for someone." Cory took a deep breath and looked her friend in the eye. "I'm scared, Kelsey. I'm scared because I know when I let myself, I will love him too much. And then he'll have control over me. I said I'd never let that happen again as long as I live."

"Oh, Cory..." Kelsey pulled Cory into a long hug. "It's not about control. Love is never about control. It's about caring and sacrifice and doing the best for each other." Kelsey drew away, bracketing Cory's face with her hands. "When you love someone you open yourself to hurt. That's what happens when you give someone your heart. But if you keep your heart to yourself, you end up old and withered and alone. Your mom went through a lot. I know that. But don't let her influence how you feel about Matthew. Please, don't."

Kelsey's pleading tone, the sincerity in her face, melted the last defense Cory had erected against Matthew. She smiled and let herself be hugged once again.

"Thanks, Kelsey. You're a true friend." Cory sniffed, blinking back a sudden surge of tears.

"Of course I am." Kelsey laughed, her own voice thick with emotion. "And you're too special to me to let this wonderful chance slip through your fingers. Trust that God wants to do good things in your life."

Chapter Twelve

"You're not coming to church?" Cory sat beside her mother on the couch, her hand resting lightly on her shoulder.

"No."

"Are you in a lot of pain today?"

"No more than usual. I don't feel like it. That's all." Joyce sighed lightly. "I know you want to be with that Matthew fellow, and I just can't sit by and watch that happen."

"Mother, stop it. I don't know why you dislike him so much."

"Yes, you do, Cory. Because one time you felt the same."

"Once I did. But he asked me to forgive him. And I have." She hesitated, knowing that she wasn't entirely sure of her own emotions in the matter. Matthew had confused her most of her life. It was only the past few days that everything felt right and true and good. Yet her feelings were so new and untried.

"I can't withhold forgiveness when it's been asked. Not when God has forgiven me so much."

Joyce sighed lightly, nodding her head. "I know, I know. But I'm worried for you." She turned to her daughter and took her hand in her own. "He's charming, Cory. Just like your dad. I made a big mistake once, Cory. Don't do the same."

Cory felt her mother's words lightly touch on her own misgivings, but refused to dwell on it.

"Our relationship, if I can dare call it that, started with him asking my forgiveness. I don't think that's a dangerous place to start from."

"Maybe not. But be careful with your heart, my dear. I know you. Once you give it, you give it all. I've had too much sorrow in my life. I want only what's best for you." Joyce reached up and stroked Cory's cheek. "You're all I've got left, Cory."

Cory laid her head on her mother's. "I love you, Mom. I always will. But you need to know that I think I really care for Matthew."

"Just be careful," she said, pressing Cory's hand against her cheek. "And say a prayer for me, would you?"

"I always do." Cory laid a gentle kiss on her mother's cheek, then got up.

"You look lovely, by the way," Joyce said, leaning back to look at her daughter. "You so seldom wear a dress."

"It looks okay?" she asked, running her hands down the clean lines of the navy shift. "I mean, it's not too dowdy, or plain?"

"Simple is always best, Cory." Joyce tilted her head to one side, considering. "You might want to add something. Just to soften the neckline. Go get that silk aqua scarf. The one I got from—'' She stopped. ''From Zeke for my birthday.''

Cory paused a moment, hearing a mixture of pain and sorrow in her voice. ''You sound sad.''

''No.'' Joyce shook her head. ''I'm not.''

''But you always sound sad when you talk about him.''

Joyce waved her away. ''Just get the scarf, and I'll tie it for you. Bring that gold pin, too.''

The subject was closed.

Cory went to her mother's bedroom, found the accessories and brought them back, sitting beside Joyce.

Joyce draped the scarf around the dress's plain neckline and pinned it carefully. ''I got this pin from your father, you know. Your real father.'' Joyce looked past Cory, as if into another place and time. ''Now he was a good man. A very good man and a good father to your brothers....'' She stopped abruptly, turning back to Cory, fussing with the scarf.

''You are thinking about the boys, aren't you?''

Joyce finished pinning the broach. ''Yes,'' she confessed. ''Yes I was. I've been thinking about them more lately. How are they doing? Are they happy? I just can't let it go.''

''Of course you can't. I think about them often, too.''

Joyce smiled. ''Wouldn't it be nice...'' She gave a short laugh. ''Wouldn't it be nice if life was easy and simple? But it isn't, Cory. You remember that.''

Cory knew she now referred to Matthew and let the comment slide. ''I'm going now, Mom. Take it easy, okay? And I hope you feel better soon.''

Joyce stroked her gently on the cheek. ''Well, my hopes are for you, Cory.''

A knock on the door broke the moment and with an eager glance over her shoulder, Cory got up. She looked back at her mother. ''I'll be praying for you,'' she said, blowing her a kiss. Then she almost flew to the door.

She pulled it open and there stood Matthew. His pose was relaxed—hands tucked into the pockets of his tan suit pants. His hair was tamed, but only slightly. But he was chewing his lower lip and the sight of his lack of confidence gave her a warm thrill.

''You look lovely,'' he said simply.

Cory fingered the scarf. ''Thanks,'' she said, unable to find anything wittier to say. ''I suppose we should go.''

Matthew tilted his head to one side, as if considering. ''Is your mother up?''

Cory glanced hesitantly back over her shoulder. ''Yes, she is.''

''Good.'' Matthew stepped inside the small porch and, taking Cory's hand, walked to the doorway of the living room. ''I just thought I would say hi, Joyce,'' he said, smiling at Joyce.

Joyce looked up, her expression neutral. ''Not only did you think it, you did it.''

''Do you mind if I take Cory out after church? Or should I bring her directly home?'' Matthew asked.

''You're probably going to do what you like, won't you?''

''No. I'm going to do what Cory wants.'' Matthew squeezed her hand and Cory felt a sudden rush of affection for him.

''Well, then, don't ask me, ask her.'' Joyce waved them off.

''I hope you have a good day,'' Matthew said.

Cory glanced at her mother and was surprised to see her expression soften, a faint smile curve her lips. In spite of her mother's animosity, Matthew's charm worked on Joyce as well. "I hope so, too," Joyce said finally. "Now you'd better go or you're going to be late."

Matthew winked at Cory, then with a tug on her hand, pulled her out the door.

Outside, he whistled lightly, swinging their joined hands as he walked down the walk. He raised his face to the sun. "This is a beautiful day, isn't it, Cory?"

She smiled at him, as he turned his head to face her. "That it is," she agreed.

They weren't late as Joyce had predicted and managed to find a place somewhere in the middle of the church. They were greeted with a few raised eyebrows, a few perceptive glances, as if some people were not surprised these two would find each other.

Once again, Cory felt self-conscious and once again Matthew took it all in stride. He greeted the people he knew and as they settled into their pew, scanned the bulletin without any apparent concern. Almost casually he slipped his arm around her, his fingers trailing on her shoulder. He glanced sidelong at her, gave her a wink and Cory relaxed.

The service began and Cory let herself be drawn along by the singing, the comfort found in the Bible readings, the encouragement from the minister's sermon.

Beside her Matthew sang easily, familiar with all the songs. He listened intently to the minister. Toward the end of the sermon, Matthew tucked Cory's arm under his, holding her hand tightly between his hands.

For the first time in many years, Cory felt contentment stealing over her. She felt as if all the anger, the confusion, and the fear had been gently wiped away by God's love and by the caring shown her by Matthew.

She felt safe. Cared for.

Just before they bowed their heads, she chanced another look at Matthew, appreciating his appeal, his charm.

Her mother's warning came back to her, darkening the moment, bringing up the few misgivings she herself harbored at times.

Please, Lord, show me that this is true, she prayed, clinging to his hand. *Show me that this is real. I want to care for him, I want to trust him. Help me.*

Slowly as she prayed she felt a gentle easing away of her misgivings. When the prayer was over, she still clung to Matthew's hand as they got up to receive the blessing. She didn't care who saw.

As they walked out of church, Cory felt someone grab her arm.

"Hey, there, Cory. How's it going?"

Cory glanced over her shoulder at Kelsey who was grinning from ear to ear. "Fine, Kelsey. Just fine," Cory said hesitantly. She hoped Kelsey would behave herself.

Kelsey glanced at Matthew with a knowing look. "I see that."

Matthew looked back and winked at Kelsey. "Good to see you again. How's the restaurant business?"

"Don't ask." Kelsey waved away his question. "So. I take it you guys don't mind coaching together for a while yet?"

"You take it correctly," Matthew said.

"Great." Kelsey grinned at the two of them. "I'd love to chat some more, but I promised Chris I would take him for a drive today. I'll see you soon, Matthew." Kelsey tapped Cory on the shoulder. "And I'll talk to you tomorrow."

Cory watched her friend go, shaking her head. "Maybe I'll call in sick," she said with a sigh.

"Why don't you?" Matthew agreed, giving her hand another squeeze. "I've got to sit in on a hearing I don't feel like going to. I'd sooner play hooky. We could spend the day together."

The slight thrill she felt at the notion of being with Matthew all day was tempered by what he said. "So you won't be in tomorrow?"

Matthew sighed and shook his head. "Afraid not. But I'll be in on Tuesday. First thing in the morning in my usual spot."

"I'll be looking for you," she said.

"I wish I didn't have to go, but life flows on." He slanted her a sideways look, his mouth curved up to one side, his dimple firmly in place.

He was such a charmer, Cory thought, her heart skipping at his surreptitious look. He turned his head, then, his expression suddenly became serious.

It was a hold-your-breath moment, she thought, still holding his hand, still surrounded by people. But for that split second there was nobody else but Matthew.

They were jostled by other churchgoers moving past them and Cory looked away. The day had become that much brighter.

"You sure you don't mind walking in those?" Matthew said, glancing down at the thin sandals Cory wore.

"It's not mountain climbing," Cory said. "I can manage."

"Okay." Matthew held out his hand to her, she took it and they started off down the secluded path.

The sun warmed their faces and now and again an imperceptible breeze cooled the air as they walked.

Matthew drew in a deep breath, a feeling of utter contentment stealing over him. The church service had been fulfilling. To have Cory share it with him had made it even more so. And now, to have her by his side made the day complete.

"I love this place." She swung their joined hands. "When we first moved here, I would come here every day after work and just walk."

"I remember meeting you here that one Sunday."

Cory glanced at him, then away. "Well, that was a while ago."

And a few events ago, he thought, remembering her animosity then. "So you've been here almost a year?"

Cory nodded, lifting her face to the sun. Her hair swung back from her face. A light flush colored her cheeks and her lips were curved in a tender smile. She was stunning, beautiful, lovely. The words could express the effect she had on him.

"Why here?" he continued, his desire to know about her also growing. "Why did you choose Stratton?"

Cory pursed her lips, looking ahead again. "We just ended up here. Whenever Mom and I would leave, we would pack up the car and head out. Take a few jogs, backtrack maybe." She gave a light shrug, as if dismissing it. "Then just go where the road took us, as far as we had money to travel. This last time it happened to be Stratton."

"Why did you always leave? Why didn't you ever stay around?" Matthew knew he was treading on shaky ground. The last time he had talked to her about Zeke, he had found out more than he wanted to. And he knew she had been holding back.

Cory took a deep breath and slowly let it out. "Why do you keep asking about him? Just let it go."

Her grip on his hand tightened and once again Matthew felt a wave of sorrow, guilt followed by intense anger. How could he and his father not have seen this part of Zeke? How could they have been so completely fooled by the man?

Matthew stopped her, pulling on her hand so that she faced him. "Cory, I just wish there was some way—" he stopped, realizing how futile his words were.

"You could change it?" Cory tilted her head to one side, as if studying him. Her expression was intent. Then she smiled lightly and traced the outline of his mouth, her touch as light as a sigh. "But then we wouldn't be here now, would we? All the things that happened brought us to this point. I believe God used it all to let this happen."

"You have such a strong faith. That amazes me considering all you've been through."

Cory looked away, drawing back, but still holding Matthew's hand. "I didn't always, you know. My mother's faith was sorely tried both after my father's death and when she had to give up the boys. Zeke about finished it. She didn't have a whole lot to pass on to me. But God found me, and for that I'm thankful."

"How did it happen?"

Cory looked away, her expression clouding as if remembering sadness.

And she had much sadness to remember, Matthew thought, slipping his arm around her shoulders protectively. He wanted to take it all away, to erase it from her life. To surround her with love and caring and kindness.

"It happened in the first town we ended up in after Zeke started intimidating us," Cory said after a long silence. "Mom and I rented a small house in town from one of the members of the local church. We hardly had anything and of course didn't tell him why. We were so scared Zeke would find us again. But soon we were inundated with furniture and clothes—all donated by the members of his church. They were so good to us. So I started going. Mom came only once in a while. She was quite bitter toward God at that time. She had lost so much."

"I realize that now," Matthew said, pulling her closer. Cory glanced up at him and smiled.

"I have to confess," she continued, "I had a hard time with church. I went because I felt I owed the people something. But I always had a hard time accepting God as my Father. The only father I had known didn't love me and didn't care for me the way a true father does. The only father I had was the one who lied to me all the time, the one who tried to hurt me. I would sit beside him listening to people reciting a prayer starting with 'Our Father' and I'd look sidelong and see Zeke. Didn't work for me. So I fought the whole idea of God and a relationship with him."

"And what made the difference?"

Cory brushed back a strand of hair from her face as she looked away. "The minister in that church had a sermon one day from Luke. Jesus lamenting for Jerusalem. The part where he says, 'How often I have longed to gather your children together, as a hen gathers her chicks under her wings,'" Cory quoted. "The idea of Jesus, God, comparing himself to something as simple as a hen. It made me laugh. But it changed my perspective. Since then I've found other passages comparing God's love to a mother, as well, that I could relate to. I still struggle with it, but I'm hoping God understands."

"I'm not surprised you struggle with seeing God as a father figure. When I first told you about Zeke's death, I thought you were rather cold and unfeeling," Matthew said quietly. "Now, knowing what I do, I'm surprised you didn't jump for joy."

Cory shrugged, drawing back from his encircling arm, taking his hand in hers. "I still can have such mixed feelings about Zeke. I still have a hard time believing that he's left me everything. Money's never been important, but I guess the gesture means something. And, of course, it's allowed me and my mother to make some real plans for the first time in our lives." She smiled up at Matthew. "You can't know how liberating that is for us. All our lives we've had to watch every penny that slipped through our fingers. Zeke's checks bounced so many times. But now," she spun around, laughing, "Now we can make all kinds of plans, dream all kinds of dreams. You've brought many good things into my life, Matthew McKnight."

Matthew's heart contracted painfully at what she said, her words underscoring the reality of the situation. He wasn't entirely sure of how she felt toward him. He wondered if her dreams and plans included him.

But the hardest part was knowing that by encouraging her to accept the will against her wishes, he had made her vulnerable to Zeke's empty promises once again.

He knew he had to tell her about the will. But when he looked down at her, into her soft brown eyes, shining with warmth and affection, when he saw how her mouth curved, felt her hand holding his, he knew he couldn't do it yet. She was here beside him. If he were to bend over and kiss her, he knew she would welcome it.

He did so, just to prove it. And she curved her hand around his neck, holding him close.

Oh, Lord, how can I tell her? Will her faith be able to withstand this? Will it turn her against You? Against me?

He couldn't bear the thought of either but the truth would come out sooner or later. The longer he waited the worse it looked for him.

Tuesday for sure, he thought. He was gone all day Monday.

He drew away, tracing her features with his finger, as if to remember them. "I care for you, Cory," he said firmly, hoping his conviction came through, hoping she would remember. "I wish I could tell you what you mean to me."

She smiled up at him. "I can't believe that my lawyer is at a loss for words," she joked.

Matthew pulled her close and kissed her again, his prayers becoming ever more fervent.

* * *

"I keep telling you, you don't have to keep McKnight hours to impress me," Nathan said, leaning in the doorway of Matthew's office early the next morning.

Matthew looked up from his computer screen and glanced at the clock on the wall. He'd been sitting in front of the computer for three hours already. His eyes felt dry and his shoulders were sore from hunching over the keyboard.

"Sorry. I didn't realize you were here," he said, stretching his arms above his head.

Nathan pushed himself away from the wall and walked farther into Matthew's office. "You don't need to apologize to me for coming in. I thought you would be getting ready for the hearing."

"I'm ready for that. I've just got a couple of other things I'm working on before I go."

"Sounds mysterious." Nathan just smiled. "My secretary tells me she's been looking up e-mail addresses of every law firm in western Canada for you. Anything I can do to help?"

Matthew shook his head. "Actually, I'm quitting for today." He thought he should tell Nathan what was he doing—that he was conducting his own search for Cory's brothers, but didn't think she would appreciate other people knowing.

He wasn't sure his initial contacts would come to anything. He had started simple—sending out a generic e-mail to any and every lawyer he had an address for to see if they had clients named Jake or Simon, last name unknown, born on such and such a date. He'd contacted Social Services who put him on to a number of agencies that helped reunite adopted children with their natural parents.

He'd used his legal contacts to put a personal ad in all the small-town western Canadian weekly newspapers through their blanket ad services. Then he had put the same ad in the major cities' dailies to be run for two weeks.

He had used his account at McKnight and McKnight to charge the ads. He didn't have a clue how much they would cost, but it didn't matter. It was a small start, but he didn't have time for much more until later on in the week.

One way or another, he was going to find these brothers for Cory.

"I saw you sitting in church with Cory Luciuk," Nathan added with an avuncular smile. "You made a nice couple. Too bad you're gone all day today."

"I know," he said softly, leaning back in his chair.

"Ah, well, absence makes the heart grow fonder. You'll see her tomorrow."

Matthew sighed, rubbing his forehead. He wished he could stifle the twinges of apprehension he felt each time he thought of seeing Cory again.

"Well, now," Nathan said with a faint smile. "You don't seem too eager about that."

Biting his lip, Matthew leaned forward. "I've got some disappointing news for her."

"I see," was all Nathan said. He tapped his thumbs together, watching Matthew. "From what I've seen, Cory has had many disappointments in her life. I'm sure she'll weather this one. She seemed pretty happy on Sunday."

Matthew wished he could be as sure as Nathan was. Nathan didn't know what Matthew did.

Nathan stood and buttoned up his coat. "I imagine you've got a few things to get ready before you go.

If you have time tonight, stop by the house and let me know how the hearing went.'' Then with a parting grin, Nathan left.

Matthew stared at the screen saver then reached over and pulled out a picture he had in his drawer.

It was a picture of Cory taken by Deirdre at their graduation. He'd had a copy of it ever since he'd seen doubles of the photo at Deirdre's place. He'd taken one, thinking she wouldn't notice. She hadn't.

For years he'd had it filed away in Zeke's file. Last week, he remembered it and asked his secretary to mail it to him.

It was the only picture he had of Cory. He couldn't help but compare it to the woman he now knew. Her face was younger in the picture, but there was a hardness around the eyes, a firmness to the mouth, that Matthew didn't see in Cory anymore.

He recalled how she had looked yesterday, how trustingly she had come to his arms and he felt almost ill.

Oh, Lord, what is she going to say? What is going to happen? He fought down a feeling of panic.

A feeling that after all this time, he was going to lose her again. All last night he had prayed, had struggled, had tried to let go.

But he kept remembering how she reacted the first time he told her about the will. How contemptuously she had said that Zeke had taught her well, not to trust any man.

And Matthew had convinced her to trust him to look out for her best interests.

But how could they have known? he argued to himself. Zeke hadn't lived in Riverview, but he hadn't instructed them any different. It wasn't uncommon for a will to be over five years old and still valid if the lawyer didn't have any further instructions.

What this woman had was a holograph will. A piece of paper written out by hand. Not registered, not documented. Just a piece of paper.

It couldn't possibly be genuine, he thought, pushing himself away from the desk. Not possibly.

He clung to that thought as he slipped into his suit coat and picked up his briefcase. He would have had time for a cup of coffee at the restaurant, but he couldn't face Cory quite yet.

Chapter Thirteen

"Thanks for coming. I hope you enjoyed your meal," Cory said as she ripped the bill off her pad and set it down on the table in front of the older couple.

They smiled their thanks and as she walked away, Cory couldn't help but look up at the clock. It was only nine twenty-five. Matthew didn't usually come in until ten, but that didn't stop her from checking, especially since he hadn't been able to come in yesterday. She'd been watching the clock for the past hour, the minute hand crawling around the face, her nervousness increasing with each increment.

It was like high school all over again, she thought with a measure of exasperation. She had dated other men before, some for more than a month, but never had she felt this way about meeting any other man.

She resisted the urge to go to the washroom and check her hair, her makeup.

Matthew had seen her in enough different circum-

stances that it shouldn't matter what she looked like
this time around.

But it did, she thought, unconsciously smoothing
her hair. A trill of apprehension shivered through her
as she once again looked out the long windows to the
street beyond.

What she saw made her stop, her expectation turning to an initial shock of fear.

A deep-green car had parked in front of the windows and as Cory watched, a tall, commanding figure
got out.

Clifton McKnight.

His grey hair was styled within a hairbreadth of
perfection. As with Matthew, the cut of his charcoal
grey suit, its crisp lines and expensive fabric easily
showed its cost. Expensive.

Clifton McKnight paused a moment, looking
around, then he closed the door and walked purpose-
fully toward the restaurant.

For Cory it was as if time had slipped back as she
once again faced those patrician features.

She swallowed against the constriction in her
throat, her palms suddenly clammy.

What was he doing here? What did he want?

She took a calming breath then, remembering that
his son worked only a couple of blocks down the
street. Of course, she reprimanded herself. He's just
come to see Matthew.

But a new wave of nerves attacked her at the
thought of meeting Clifton now. Now that she and
Matthew had spent time together.

What would Clifton think of her? Would he think
she wasn't good enough for his son? She had always
known what Clifton thought of her and her mother.

She didn't imagine that things had changed. Clifton McKnight would want only the best for his only son.

The door opened and Clifton stepped into the restaurant and it was as if everything slowed, turned and became centered on him. His presence was always commanding, thought Cory, taking a step back behind one of the partitions.

She wasn't hiding, she told herself. She just needed a few moments to compose herself. To catch the breath that always eluded her in his presence.

Clifton walked toward the first empty table and sat down. He folded his hands on the table in front of him looking around, his expression carefully neutral.

From where she stood, Cory could easily see the resemblance between him and Matthew. The same level brows, the slightly angled eyes, giving both Clifton and Matthew a deceptively languid look.

But where Matthew had charm, Clifton had presence.

Please, Lord, help me through this, she prayed, pressing her hand against her stomach as if to still the flurry of nerves. *I know who I am, that You love me. But I have always been afraid of this man.*

The door chimes sounded again, and Cory glanced quickly at the door.

Her heart fluttered this time at the sight of Matthew glancing around the restaurant. She could tell the instant he spotted his father.

He paused a moment, smoothed his hand over his slightly unruly hair, straightened his coat, squared his shoulders and walked over to where his father sat.

Cory wanted to rush over. Wanted to drag Matthew away from his father, to break the tableau she was now witnessing.

Clifton standing up, shaking hands with his son, then giving him a quick, manly hug.

Matthew smiling back at his father as they both sat down.

Father and son, together again.

It called back a horrible time in her life. It brought back even more vividly the feelings of lack of control. Of powerlessness, seeing them together.

She wanted to leave, but they were sitting at her table. So she took a long, slow, calming breath and walked toward them portraying a confidence she didn't feel, struggling to bring the present to the moment.

"Hello, Matthew," she said quietly, then turned to Clifton. "Mr. McKnight."

"Hi, Cory," Matthew smiled up at her, then looked across the table to his father. "Dad, I'm sure you remember Cory Smith?" Matthew glanced up at her, then away as he corrected himself. "Sorry. Cory Luciuk."

Matthew seemed uneasy and Cory wondered if it was his father's presence.

Clifton gave Cory a curt nod. "Yes, I remember Cory," he said. "How are you doing?"

His deep voice resonated through her mind, pulling back all the ugly memories that she had fought to bury.

"I'm fine," she replied, unable to make her voice get any louder than a faint rasp. She cleared her throat and tried again.

"By the way, I'd like to offer my condolences on the death of your stepfather."

Cory gave him a wan smile, accepting his sympathy. She was on shaky ground and was determined to get back some of the home ice advantage. "Can I get you some coffee?" she said with more confidence than she felt.

"Yes. That sounds good," Clifton said. "Coffee for both of us." Clifton looked back at her. "Do you have some time, Cory? There's something I need to discuss with you."

Cory felt her heart thud to a halt, then race away. What could Clifton possibly have to tell her? "I've got a coffee break coming in about ten minutes, but I could take it early."

Clifton acknowledged that with a curt nod.

Cory looked at Matthew, willing him to glance up at her again, to give her some kind of hint what his father wanted. Matthew's early arrival at the restaurant showed her that this meeting had been arranged. But why?

She wanted him to smile at her, tell her that everything was all right. More than ever, in the presence of his father and the past, she needed some kind of assurance that he was the same Matthew who had called her last night, who had teased and laughed with her.

But sitting across from his father, he could barely acknowledge her presence. It was as if he were ashamed of her.

Swallowing down a building knot of sorrow and apprehension, she turned, got the coffee and came quickly back.

Without saying a word she poured them each a cup, her cheeks hot with shame and confusion. How was she supposed to calmly sit with both of them and discuss whatever it was Clifton wanted to talk about?

Matthew was suddenly distant, Clifton looked as

imperious as ever. Once again she felt like the rebellious girl they didn't think much of, the girl who caused them nothing but trouble.

She brought the coffeepot back, and just before she returned to the table, grabbed the edge of the counter, her eyes shut tight.

I don't know what is happening, Lord, she prayed, *but I feel scared, confused. I feel like Matthew doesn't want to see me. It hurts. Please take the hurt away. Help me to trust in You, that You will take care of me.*

She didn't want to go back, wanted to stay in this place, talking to God who she knew loved her unconditionally.

But practicality intervened. Smoothing down her hair and sucking in a quick breath, she turned, lifted her head and walked back to the table.

Matthew looked up as she came closer, his expression guarded.

Ignoring him, Cory sat down in the chair across from Clifton, matching his level gaze, stare for stare.

"You wished to talk to me," she said, her voice level, even, not even betraying the emotions that twisted beneath the facade of calm.

Clifton gave Matthew a quick look, then looked back at Cory. "I'm presuming Matthew told you about the problem we had with Zeke's will."

Cory shook her head. Matthew had said nothing about the will.

He wouldn't look at her, and she felt an ominous pounding beginning in her head. She couldn't talk, couldn't say anything, willing Clifton to continue.

Clifton cleared his throat and pushed his coffee cup aside, resting his forearms on the table. "I thought the will would be probated quite quickly. I was wrong. I hadn't seen Zeke for approximately a year before his death and apparently he met another woman whom he had been living with.''

Clifton paused, his head tilting to one side, his expression softening as he continued. ''In that time period, he drew up another will. It's what we call a holograph will—it was witnessed, signed and dated.''

Icy fingers gripped her forehead and hands. She almost swayed, but caught the table, stopping herself. Don't let them see, she thought, reverting back to what she called her survival techniques. Don't let them know how they've gotten to you. Don't let them think they've won.

''And what does that mean for me?'' Her voice came out calm, quiet and for that she was grateful.

''It could mean that the will in which you were named beneficiary could be declared invalid.''

She felt Matthew rest his hand on her arm but she pulled it back as Clifton's words registered. Zeke hadn't left her anything after all. Another wrapped-up box that was empty when opened. Like always.

How long had Matthew known about this other will? How long had he kept this information to himself? Why didn't he prepare her? Tell her?

''What are you going to do?'' she asked Clifton, her voice portraying a calm she didn't feel.

''We can fight it. The will was handwritten. We could debate the soundness of his mind at the time, whether he actually wrote the will or not. There's a number of angles we could take.''

''And how would I pay for this?''

''Any legitimate challenges to the estate would be drawn from the estate itself.''

Cory absorbed this for a moment, then threw Clifton a wary look. "And the longer the fight goes on, the higher the lawyers' bills. A challenge could conceivably drain the estate until there is nothing left to fight over, right?"

"You're very astute," Clifton said with a hint of admiration in his voice. "That is a possibility. Sometimes both parties can agree to a fair and equitable distribution before that happens."

"Do you think that can happen?"

Clifton was quiet a moment, then looked her straight in the eye. "No. The other woman wants her full share of the estate."

Cory let the words register as her eyes slid away from his. Then, slowly, the old familiar anger ignited deep within her.

Zeke had betrayed her once again. And Matthew had encouraged her to put herself in this position. He hadn't told her the truth.

"None of this should surprise me," she said pushing her chair back and getting to her feet, forcing a calm she didn't feel. "I never wanted anything from Zeke from the first. I didn't trust him, and I was right not to. I was misled."

Then without looking at Matthew, she turned and walked away, ignoring his calls to wait.

She ducked around a partition and pulled off her apron as she strode toward the kitchen. She didn't know where she was going. All she knew was that she had to get away, to be alone.

Matthew caught up to her just before she reached the back door leading out of the restaurant.

"Cory, please listen to me."

She turned to him, her anger now white-hot, the sting of Zeke's treachery sharp in it's familiarity.

"No. You listen to me. I told you I didn't want anything from that stupid will in the first place. You told me to sign it, told me that maybe Zeke wanted to make things up to me. If I hadn't done that I would have never ended up feeling like this again. Like maybe, somehow he wanted...wanted..." And then to her shame, her voice broke off.

"Cory, I'm sorry." He held out his hand as if to touch her, but she moved away from him.

"I never wanted anything from him, but you said it would be different." She lashed out, part of her crying out to stop, but she couldn't. It was too familiar, the pain, the betrayal. The lies. "All my life, I've wanted a father, someone who would love me. He was the only father I ever knew. And he hated me."

Tears gathered, filling her eyes, but she couldn't stop now. She had let down too many barriers with Matthew and she couldn't hold back what she had to say.

"Do you know what it's like to live with someone who wants only to hurt you, and all you want is someone to love you?" She stopped, shaking her head, glancing over his shoulder at his father. "Of course you don't. Your father only wanted the best for you, gave you everything you ever needed or wanted. All I ever wanted from Zeke was some expression of love. Some way of knowing that somehow I was important to him. That I mattered. I spent years building up my defenses against him. Years. And now, in just a few weeks, you helped me break them down." She stared at Matthew, unaware of the tears coursing down her cheeks.

"I'm sorry," he said quietly. He reached out for her again, but she couldn't bear to have him touch her.

"Leave me alone, McKnight. You were his lawyer." With another sob she turned and ran out of the door.

Once outside, she began to run, unsure of where she was going, only knowing that she had to get away from Matthew and the memories.

She didn't stop until she got to the river.

Panting with exertion she leaned back against a tree. Thoughts, memories whirled, converging until she couldn't control herself. She covered her face in her hands and wept angry, bitter tears, her shoulders shaking with the strength of her sorrow.

When the worst storm had passed, she wiped her eyes, laying her head back against the rough bark of the tree wondering how she could have been so stupid.

Just a few days ago she had foolishly told Matthew that she believed God had brought them to this place. That her life had reached some kind of happy ending thanks to the will. What a sap she had been. It was all a lie. Zeke had once again hurt her. Betrayed her.

And Matthew knew all along.

Had he known when he came to Stratton? Had he used the will as some kind of bargaining chip to get close to her? Was everything he told her a lie?

Was he as manipulative as Zeke was? He was a man, wasn't he? Once he had defended her stepfather, believed him.

But Matthew told her that he believed her.

Was that more lies?

Questions came at her from all angles, voicing all the doubts she had quenched because she believed his words. Had fallen for his charm. Just as her mother warned her.

Sliding against the tree, she lowered herself to the ground. Objections and suspicions all spun through her head unable to find a coherent center; pain and anger twisted her stomach. She didn't know what to feel, what to think.

She wanted to pray, but every time she started, the only line that would come to her was, "Our Father..."

As she had told Matthew, she had never received love from a father. And now it seemed that even God was in on the joke on her. She had asked for all this, she thought, wrapping her arms around her knees, pressing her face against them. She who knew better, had gone against the better judgment that had been hard-won through many confrontations with Zeke Smith.

No one else had been the dupe but her.

She squeezed her eyes shut, as another sob shook her. Foolish, foolish woman. What have you done?

Cory allowed herself the questions, the anger, the sorrow. She let it all roll over her. Then, wiping away the tears from her cheeks, she opened her eyes.

The trees covered the sky, like a canopy overhead. Through their green leaves the sun filtered. A curious squirrel chirped from a branch, then scampered away.

"Life goes on," Cory muttered. "It just keeps on going."

She knew that's what she had to do. Keep going.

How and where she was supposed to head from here, she didn't know.

And what about Matthew?

Wasn't love supposed to be built on trust? How could she trust him now? Her heart contracted painfully as she thought of him. She didn't know what to do.

"I take it you hadn't told her about the other will yet," Clifton said as Matthew came back to where his father sat. When his father had unexpectedly called to tell him he was coming, Matthew assumed it was for a visit. He was as surprised as Cory when Clifton brought up the will.

"No, I hadn't," Matthew said heavily, dropping into the chair. He wasn't so sure he had done the right thing in letting Cory leave. Not in her state, but he was afraid of what would happen if he went after her.

She didn't trust him anymore. What a mess he had made of everything by waiting. By selfishly thinking that they needed time together.

"Why hadn't you told her?"

Matthew resented his father's probing. Mostly because he knew he had been in the wrong. "I wanted to wait for the right time," he said with a resigned sigh. "I realized when I got your call to meet you here that I had waited too long." He massaged his forehead with his fingers as he remembered what she had said about wanting a father's love. His heart twisted at the memory. She had grown up with so much pain and disappointment. And now, thanks to his urging, she had been put in that position once again.

Clifton was silent a moment, sipping his coffee

thoughtfully. "She's as emotional as ever," he said finally.

Matthew glanced up at his father to see if he was joking, but Clifton looked dead serious. "She's had a lot to be emotional about," Matthew said flatly. "Cory told me her side of the living-with-Zeke-Smith story." Matthew held his father's gaze, his own steady. "Zeke was a manipulative fraud, Dad. Cory was just a means to an end, and the end was to win against Joyce. Which he did thanks to us. And now, thanks to us, thanks to me," he corrected, "she allowed herself to be beaten by him again."

"It was an unforeseen error," Clifton said. "There was no way we could have known about that will. You approached her in good faith."

"I don't think that will was so unforseen," Matthew snapped. "I wouldn't be surprised if he set the whole thing up." Then in succinct words, sparing no details, he told his father what Cory had told him.

"We were fooled by him," Matthew said finally. "Both of us. And Cory and Joyce had to pay a high price for that."

Clifton sat back, his expression betraying his incredulity. "But this was the very thing we fought against in court. Her words against Zeke's. I've known Zeke for years. We've gone golfing together, spent time together. He always talked about her, how much he cared for her…" He rested his head on his fingertips, confusion threading through his voice. "How do you know she's right?"

"Because I just feel in my heart that she's right." Matthew plunged his hands through his hair. "I would think this last little business with the will would be enough to convince both of us that she told me the truth. And now she's out there somewhere, hating me, you and Zeke. We're all one package to her, and it rips me apart inside to have her think that I'm anything like that man.''

Matthew ran his hand over his face in a gesture of resignation. "She told me to leave her alone, but I can't." He looked at his father. "To know that she hates me hurts more than anything I've ever felt.''

Clifton's expression was sorrowful, his touch gentle as he reached across the table to clasp his son's arm. "I'm sorry, Matthew. I feel like I'm responsible for all of this. I should have told you why I was coming, but I assumed you had told her about the will already.''

"I should have," Matthew said with a sigh. "But I was afraid she would do exactly what she did right now. I thought I would give us a chance. Buy us some time. The only trouble is, right now it hurts me more.''

Clifton was quiet a moment, regarding his son with a thoughtful stare. "I get the feeling she means a lot to you.''

Matthew laughed shortly. "More than a lot, Dad." He looked directly at his father and taking a slow breath decided it was time to tell him. "I'm thinking of staying here. Staying in Stratton and taking over Nathan's practice.''

To the casual observer, Clifton's expression never changed. But Matthew could see his father's lips thin, the faint tightening of the muscles in his face. "Because of her?''

"*Her* name is Cory," Matthew said quietly. "And yes, she is one of the reasons I'm staying here. The others we've talked about endlessly before. I like it here, I like the pace of the work, I like the kind of work. I don't feel like I'm racing, trying forever to maintain the family reputation.'' He didn't want to say anything about his father's marriage. That wasn't really relevant to the discussion, but he also knew he wanted to be able to have the same kind of relationship with his wife that Nathan had with Mary.

And a relationship like that took the investment of time.

''She means that much to you, Matthew?''

''I love her,'' Matthew said with a short laugh, as if doubting his own feelings. ''Although I don't know where I stand with her now.''

Clifton leaned back, his hands resting on the edge of the table. ''Then I suggest you have some work to do, Matthew. If you truly care for her.''

Chapter Fourteen

The shrill sound of the phone ringing greeted Cory as she stepped into her house. The demanding noise cut through her.

She ignored it. It was probably Matthew and she didn't want to talk to him. If it was anyone else, well, she didn't want to talk to them, either.

"Can you get that please?" Joyce called from the kitchen.

Cory hesitated a moment, then praying it was just a routine call, picked it up.

"Cory, don't hang up," she heard the voice on the other end say.

It was Matthew after all.

"I don't have anything to say to you," she said dispiritedly. "Please leave me alone." She had no reserves to deal with him, no way of resisting him.

"Cory, don't do this. Don't push me away. I'm sorry. I should have told you...."

Cory pressed her fingertips to eyes still tender from

crying as she slowly sat down on the couch. "I can't deal with you right now, Matthew."

"What do you mean?"

Cory wished she were better with words. Wished she could explain the confusion, the convoluted emotions that she couldn't untangle herself. Matthew and his father and Zeke, all intertwined. All had created unhappiness in her life. All had betrayed her in one way or another. How could she separate Matthew from that? How could she explain it to him when she wasn't sure herself?

"Cory, I need to talk to you. Please let me come over."

Cory felt a sob rise in her throat. She glanced up to see her mother standing in the doorway of the kitchen. And how was she going to tell Joyce that once again Zeke had taken something away from them?

She didn't want Matthew to witness her pain. So she hung up.

"Who was that, dear?" Joyce asked with a frown.

"Wrong number," Cory answered, pulling her legs up to her chest, as if to protect her heart.

"What's the matter?" Joyce came into the living room and sat down on the couch beside her daughter. "Are you feeling okay?"

"I'm tired," Cory said quietly.

Joyce touched Cory's forehead. "You don't feel hot, or flushed, yet your cheeks are red."

Cory studied her mother's face, noting the lines etched by disappointment, deepened by the pain her mother dealt with every day. "If you had one wish, Mom, what would it be?"

Joyce tilted her head sideways, studying Cory. "What brought this on?"

Cory shrugged. "Just wondering."

"Well, I think you know the answer to that." Joyce held Cory's gaze, a light smile playing around her mouth.

"The boys," Cory said softly.

"Yes, I'd like to know about them, but you are my main concern, Cory. Always have been." Joyce lightly brushed a strand of hair away from Cory's face, tucking it carefully behind her ear. "My wish would be that you would be free to do whatever you wanted. To make your own choices. I've often felt like a burden to you. Like you've had to take care of me."

"No, don't say that," Cory protested.

"Let me finish. I sometimes wish there were a way I could let you live your life." Joyce smiled lightly. "When you first told me about this will, I didn't want you to take anything from Zeke. But now, I'm glad you decided to go ahead. Because it will mean that maybe you will have a chance to finally do what you want to do."

Each quiet word cut through Cory, twisting and reinforcing her distress. How could she have been so blind, so naive as to put them both in this position once again? Once again her mother would have to face disappointment.

"I don't know how to tell you this, Mom," Cory said, straightening. "But I just got back from seeing Matthew and his father. There was another will that surfaced later. We aren't going to get anything from Zeke after all."

Joyce sat back, puzzled. "What do you mean?"

Even as Joyce voiced the question, Cory could see resignation on her face. "The will giving everything to me isn't valid anymore because some woman Zeke was living with showed up with a handwritten will leaving her everything. We could fight it but that would mean more lawyers' fees and more hassle."

"You don't want to do that, do you?"

Cory shook her head. "No. I don't. She can have it. I knew I should never have believed Matthew in the first place." Her words sounded so harsh and even as she spoke them, Cory knew that they weren't entirely true.

But when the phone rang again, neither she nor her mother answered it.

Matthew set the phone carefully in the cradle and blew out his breath. Well, that was a bust. He knew he shouldn't expect that Cory would fall willingly into his arms after what had happened this afternoon.

But he had hoped, prayed she might at least listen. Even just for a moment.

He sat back in his chair, swiveling back and forth, back and forth as he considered his options. How could he reach her? How could he tell her that he was just plain ordinary Matthew, a man desperately in love with her? A man who had made a mistake with far-reaching consequences.

A rush of fear coursed through him at the thought that she might bolt. That once again she and Joyce might decide to up and leave. He could just imagine what Cory's mother was saying to her right now.

Please, Lord. I love her. Show me how to help her. Show her that she's wrong about me.

He dragged his hands over his face, considering his

options. He could go straight over to her house right now and try to convince her, but if he couldn't do it over the phone, he doubted he could tell her in front of her mother.

He could wait, but for what?

For now, however, he had work to do. His clients wouldn't accept the excuse of his mixed-up love life for not moving forward on their work.

He pulled open a file he had been working on and tried to focus, tried to think about his work. But all he could see was Cory's dark-brown eyes, shining with tears of hurt and betrayal. All he could hear was her longing for love from a man who had hurt her so badly.

He slammed the folder shut, furious with Zeke, hurting for Cory.

He dropped his head into his hands, his heart sore for the woman he loved, wishing he knew how to help her.

Get her through this time, Lord, he prayed. *Help her to get over this disappointment, this feeling of being betrayed once again. Show her that Your love for her is perfect even if the love we poor human beings try to give her isn't.* He drew in a slow breath, willing away the fear that she was slipping away from him.

And as he thought, he slowly figured out how to start wooing back the woman he loved.

His thoughts were broken by the sound of his secretary's voice coming over the intercom.

"I've got a Mr. Kowalchuk on the line for you, Matthew," she said.

He sighed and leaned closer to his intercom. "I'll take the call." He wasn't getting anything else done.

A few moments later Matthew hung up the phone with a mixture of anticipation threaded through with apprehension. Mr. Kowalchuk was the lawyer for a certain Jake Steele who was the brother of Simon Steele. Mr. Kowalchuk had just read Matthew's e-mail.

It turned out that some time ago, Jake had instructed Mr. Kowalchuk to see if he could find a mother and daughter named Joyce and Cory Smith.

Mr. Kowalchuk was positive that his clients were looking for Matthew's.

Life goes on, life goes on. This refrain sung through Cory's head over the next two days. She managed to smile at the customers, throw out a few lame jokes, but each time the door opened, she jumped, half dreading, half anticipating Matthew's arrival.

But he never did come either day. And she didn't know whether to feel relieved or whether to cry.

It was as if her emotions were in suspension. She held herself close, afraid to examine how she truly felt.

She relived the scene with Clifton and Matthew again and again, unable to stop.

She had overreacted.

She had done the right thing.

Matthew had hidden the truth from her.

Matthew had asked her forgiveness.

The last thought always made her stop. Always made her recognize that Matthew believed her. Cared for her.

Home was hardly sanctuary, either. Her mother was

irritable and cranky, muttering loudly about sneaky lawyers, reinforcing Cory's own doubts.

By midafternoon of the second day Matthew still hadn't come. The four aspirin she had taken were finally taking effect when Kelsey met up with Cory in the kitchen.

"Can you come to my office?" Kelsey stood in front of her friend, her arms crossed over her chest with a no-nonsense look on her face.

Cory glanced at the clock. "I've got an hour to go yet. I'll finish my shift."

"I don't care. You look miserable."

"Please, Kelsey. I just don't want to talk right now."

"You've messed up two orders already. I think you may as well come and have a cup of coffee with me." Kelsey caught her friend by the arm and almost dragged her to her office.

"Sit down. Tell Aunty Kelsey why you've been walking around with rings under your eyes, looking like you're ready to burst into tears. I heard that Matthew and his dad came in the day before yesterday and that you took off after that. I don't think I'm being too snoopy to ask you why. I wanted to talk to you yesterday already, but figured you needed some time to yourself."

Cory leaned her chair back against the wall, closing her eyes in resignation. Once again Kelsey was acting as her confessor and once again it was a relief to talk to her. "One of these days remind me to tell you how bossy you are," Cory complained.

"I'm your friend," Kelsey said quietly.

Cory opened her eyes and smiled sadly. "That you

are. And I don't know if I've ever told you how thankful I am for that friendship.''

''You've told me now.'' Kelsey tilted her head to one side. ''So. What happened?''

''Clifton McKnight came to tell me that there was another will. That means Mom and I don't get anything.''

''Oh, Cory. I'm sorry.''

''Me, too. The worst of it was, Matthew knew about it for a week and didn't tell me.'' Cory lifted her hand in puzzlement. ''Why didn't Matthew tell me? What was he trying to do? Protect that lousy ex-stepfather of mine?''

''Maybe Matthew was scared to tell you.''

''And why would that be?''

''Because of the way you're acting right now.''

Cory dropped the chair's front legs back on the floor. ''Matthew has never been scared of anything in his life.''

''I think he's scared of you.''

Cory felt a slight shiver at what Kelsey said. ''Don't be ridiculous.''

Kelsey leaned against her desk, her hands resting behind her. ''I see how he looks at you, Cory. The man is crazy for you.''

Cory shook her head. ''Then why didn't he come yesterday or today?''

''What do you want, Cory? You're angry with him yet you want him to come here so that you can give him the cold shoulder?''

''No, that's not it.''

''Oh, you'd sooner he stayed away so you can brood about how awful men are? So you can convince yourself that you don't deserve love? That you don't deserve to be happy?''

Cory glared at Kelsey, but couldn't reply.

''Don't do this, Cory. Don't push him away. He's a great guy and you know it.''

Cory wished she could make things as easy as Kelsey did. She wished she could neatly sort out her emotions and label them Past and Present.

''What do you want, Cory?'' Kelsey asked.

Cory dropped her face in her hands. ''I don't know how to explain it.''

''Why don't you try to tell me?''

Cory swallowed down a thick knot of pain, searching for the right words. She had never had a true friend like Kelsey, had never opened herself up to anyone before. Not even her mother. All her life she had been the strong one.

''Cory. You just told me that I'm your friend,'' Kelsey said quietly, her voice inviting affinity. ''You're right. I care about you. I've been praying for you. Praying for good things for you. Please, tell me.''

Cory took a deep breath, lowering her hands, smiling back at her friend. ''You won't think I'm crazy?''

''Cory. Please.''

''I'm just so confused,'' she said finally. ''I can't pray, I can't think. I love Matthew, but I'm scared. I'm scared of what he can do to me. I didn't even love my stepfather as much as I love Matthew and if Zeke can hurt me this much even after he's dead, how much more can Matthew?''

''But he cares about you, Cory. I know he does. He would do anything for you.''

''I'm scared to trust him, Kelsey. He lied to me.''

Kelsey slowly shrugged as she considered what Cory said. "I think he was trying to protect you. That's all. Maybe it wasn't right. But I don't think it was so terribly wrong." Kelsey leaned forward, her gaze intent. "Don't give up on him. I know you care deeply for each other."

They were interrupted by a sharp knock on the door.

Kelsey got up and answered it then turned to Cory.

"Some guy is here with a parcel for you." Kelsey stepped aside.

A man in a uniform entered. "Cory Luciuk?" he said, glancing at his clipboard and then at her.

"That's me."

"Parcel delivery." He handed Cory the clipboard indicating where she was to sign. Kelsey already had the parcel and had set it on her desk.

"Who is this from?" Cory asked, curiosity getting the best of her.

"It says—" the man tilted the clipboard "—Matthew. That's all."

Cory swallowed, her breath suddenly quickening.

He ripped a sheet off, folded it in half and handed it to her. Then he left.

Kelsey picked up the brown-wrapped parcel and held it out to her. "Open it, girl."

Almost hesitantly she took it, wondering what it could possibly be.

It was a large box, but not heavy. She gave it a tentative shake, puzzled.

"Cory, quit this. Open it already." Kelsey handed her a pair of scissors.

Carefully, Cory cut away the brown paper, surprised to find another layer of bright, colored wrapping paper beneath that.

"It looks too pretty to unwrap," she said, almost breathless. It looked festive and promising.

Her heart's rhythm changed and for a moment she just held the box in her hands, testing its weight, surprised at how clammy her palms were. Carefully, with delicate precision, she peeled the tape off, careful not to rip the shiny paper.

For a moment she was a child, delaying the pleasure, letting the anticipation linger. Then, just before she peeled back the paper, to her dismay, she saw her fingers tremble.

Other images came to mind. The same feeling of anticipation, the sense of wonder mingled with curiosity. And then, the letdown.

For a brief moment, she didn't dare to unwrap it further, to feel the hollow drop of disappointment.

Then, as if in defiance of the memories, she roughly pushed the paper back to reveal a box, its front covered with clear plastic. A doll box.

She lifted it up to look better. Deep-green eyes fringed with thick eyelashes stared back at her from the most delicate doll's face Cory had ever seen.

Unable to suppress the gasp of pleasure, she slowly took in all its features. Her lips were slightly pouted, painted a shiny red, her cheeks delicately blushed.

Shiny auburn curls framed her face, held back on one side with a cluster of cream-colored silk rosebuds.

Her dress was of deep-green velvet and trimmed with the same silk roses, delicate lace and the narrowest of ribbon. She wore stockings and a pair of patent leather shoes complete with tiny buckles.

She was the most exquisite doll Cory had ever seen.

"Oh, Cory. She's gorgeous," Kelsey breathed. But underlying the sense of wonder, Cory heard her puzzlement.

A doll wasn't the kind of gift a man gives a woman important to him.

But as Cory held the box, she remembered what she had told Matthew. She knew exactly what he was trying to say. Her heart fluttered as she thought of the implications. "I know what it means," she said softly.

"There's something inside," Kelsey said.

Cory saw it, too, and carefully opened the box and pulled out the envelope. Ripping it open she pulled out a card decorated with flowers.

Slowly she opened the card.

"'Dear Cory,'" she read, "'I'm sorry I hurt you. I was scared to tell you about the will. I let you down. I'm sorry. I can't promise to never let you down again, but I can promise to try not to. I love you.'"

She felt new tears well up in her eyes as she read his words.

Carefully she closed the card and slipped it back into the envelope, sniffing. Kelsey handed her a tissue and she wiped the tears away, blew her nose.

"Why don't you go home?"

Cory drew in a slow breath. "I don't want to."

"Why not?"

Cory looked up at her friend. "Because at home I get to listen to my mother saying she was right all along about Matthew. About men. That they are not to be trusted. It's so hard to hear and when I'm with her I wonder if I'm being fooled again."

"Then listen to me. Your friend. I know you love Matthew. I know he loves you. Let go of your mistrust and what your stepfather has done. He is just one man. Trust that maybe God wants to give you something good. You're allowed to take things when they're given to you. You just have to remember who the giver is."

Cory wanted too badly to believe her friend, and took comfort from the conviction in Kelsey's voice. And in that moment she realized how few times in her life she had allowed herself to take. To receive.

Holding the box close to her, Cory stood.

"And maybe when you're home," Kelsey continued, "you might want to give that poor, suffering man a call." Kelsey balled up the paper and shook her head. "And you could ask him, from me, why a doll?"

In spite of her sorrow, Cory laughed. She knew why. "Thanks. You're a true friend."

"My only concern is for you, Cory. You know that. Let yourself be happy."

Cory thought of what Kelsey told her as she got into her car, as she set the doll on the seat beside her. She drove away from the restaurant and, on a whim, took a detour past the park where Matthew had met her for the first time.

She got out and walked over to the picnic table where she had heard that Zeke Smith was dead. That he was no longer a part of her and her mother's lives.

How much had changed since that day, she thought, looking around.

She lowered her head into her hands and began to pray. She didn't know what to say, or how to say it. So she simply opened her heart to God, let Him understand what she felt. Her confusion. Her fear. *I know Your love is perfect,* she prayed. *I know You want to give. Teach me to take. Teach me to receive.*

God's love was perfect, untainted by human emotions and once again she let that love heal her.

Once again tears slipped down her cheeks, but this time they were tears of healing.

She let the moment cleanse her and then, getting up from the picnic bench, she knew what she had to do.

Chapter Fifteen

"**I**s Cory there?" Matthew asked when Kelsey answered the phone.

"She just left." Kelsey paused a moment. "She got your package, by the way. I don't know if this is how lawyers go courting, but where I come from flowers is usually the way to go."

"What did she say?"

"You made her cry and you made her smile."

Matthew's heart contracted at that.

"She also said that she knew what it meant." Kelsey snorted. "Honestly you two have the strangest courtship going."

"Was she happy at all?"

"Matthew that poor woman is eating her heart out for you. Only she's scared to admit it. Why don't you mosey on over to her house and talk to her yourself?"

"I just might do that. Thanks a lot." He set the phone down, glancing at the clock. It was a bit early to call it a day, but what he wanted to do rated above setting up a will for Alison and Jeffrey Scott.

He paused, then went back to the phone. He had to know before he went.

He punched in the numbers, praying as he did. Praying that Cory would listen.

Each ring of the phone increased his own trepidation. Then finally...

"Hello."

Strange that only one mundane word from her could create that funny breathless feeling in him.

"This is Matthew," he said, leaning back against the desk for support.

Silence.

"Please don't hang up. Please let me talk to you."

"I won't hang up," she said softly.

"Cory, honey. I'm sorry. Again." He laughed a humorless laugh as he clutched the phone. "I should have told you about that other will, but I was scared."

"Really?"

"Yes. Really. I'm as human as the next guy in love, Cory. I was afraid that you would get angry."

"I did, didn't I?"

He smiled at that. And for the first time in two days felt a glimmer of hope. "I should have told you."

"It didn't really change anything, did it? Waiting to tell me."

"But it wasn't fair. I let you hope. Every time I heard you talk about the money from the will, I felt sick. It was wrong."

"Well, I'm over it. I should have known better."

He paused, wondering. "Did you get my parcel?"

"Oh, Matthew, she's so beautiful." He heard her draw in a slow breath. "Not just because it was a present...but because I know what you were trying to say."

"I didn't know how else to say it. I want to give you everything that's in my power to give you—" He stopped, surprised at the hitch in his own voice, unable to tell her what she really meant to him. "I love you," he said simply, "And I'd like to come over."

"Please. Please come over."

"I'll be right there."

He waited for her to hang up but he could still hear her breathing. "You have to hang up," he said.

She laughed. "I remember Deirdre doing this with her boyfriend. I always thought that was silly."

"It is," he agreed.

"Then you hang up first. Otherwise you can't come over."

This time he laughed. "I love you, Cory." With a deep, slow sigh, he laid the phone in its cradle, sent up a heartfelt prayer of thanks and pushed away from his desk.

He caught his coat from the back of the chair, and slipped it on, tightened the knot on his tie, ran a hand over his usually unruly hair and just as he was about to step out of his office, the intercom buzzed.

Stifling an irritable sigh, he walked over.

"What is it?"

"I've got two men who would like to see you. They don't have an appointment. Jake and Simon Steele."

Matthew paused, surprise bolting through him. He had just talked to Jake's lawyer yesterday and now they were already here.

Their timing was atrocious. All he needed was one more day. Twenty-four hours to fix up this mess between him and Cory without any other distractions.

But he wasn't even going to get a couple of hours with her. He stifled his own impatience, realizing he was being selfish. For Cory, these were the men she had been thinking of much of her life.

For Joyce, the sons that necessity and difficult circumstances had forced her to give up. It was a momentous occasion.

Thank you, Lord, he breathed, forcing his own concerns aside.

"Okay. I'll be right out," he said.

Matthew readjusted his tie and glanced down at his clothes, surprised that he should feel suddenly nervous.

Cory's brothers.

He pushed open the door and taking a deep breath walked out into the waiting area.

Two men were standing by the window who turned as he came closer. They didn't look alike, but in Matthew's first impression he could see Cory in both of them. The tallest one was dark, his eyes the same deep brown as Cory's, holding the same wariness. The other had sandy-brown hair, the same color as Cory's. His mouth had the same mocking tilt that Cory's could.

There was no doubt in Matthew's mind who these two men were.

"Hello. I'm Matthew McKnight." Matthew held out his hand toward the tallest man.

"Jake Steele." Jake's hand in Matthew's was hard and callused. "This is my brother, Simon."

"We understand you know Cory and our mother," Simon said as he returned Matthew's handshake.

"Yes. They live here in Stratton. Have for the past few months. If I had known you were coming…"

Simon glanced at Jake, then back at Matthew. "We should have called, but I'm the impulsive one and wanted to come out right away. We've had a few disappointments already, that's why we thought it would be best if we talked to you first, before going to see them."

Matthew acknowledged this with a nod. "I understand. Would you like to come into my office a moment? There's a few things I would like to go over with you."

Even though he could see a family resemblance he wasn't about to bring two completely unknown men to Cory and Joyce's place. Not when so much emotion was at stake. And especially not after the last disappointment Cory had just suffered.

Once inside Matthew's office, Jake handed Matthew a letter. "This is from my lawyer. Just to let you know that we're on the level. We didn't want to go directly to their house. You have to understand that this is a difficult situation for us, as well." Jake glanced at Simon. "As Simon said, we've had our share of disappointments and false leads. When my lawyer told us that you knew Cory and Joyce, we thought this time we would take things a little slower."

Considering they were here only a day after Matthew had spoken to Jake's lawyer, he thought they were moving quick enough.

Matthew glanced at the paper, then back at the brothers. "This looks in order. I spoke with Mr. Kowalchuk yesterday."

"Are you Cory and Joyce's legal representative?" Simon asked warily.

Matthew thought of the will and the attendant proceedings and decided to stretch the truth a little. It was for Cory's sake, he reminded himself. "Yes, I am. Now, the question is, how do you want to proceed on this?"

Simon glanced at Jake, then back at Matthew. "We were hoping that you, or someone from this office, would be able to take us to their home."

"They are still living here, aren't they?" Jake asked.

"Yes, they are," Matthew replied. "In fact, I just found out Cory got off work early and is home right now."

The brothers exchanged another quick glance. Matthew could sense their banked anticipation and felt a flash of jealousy.

How excited Cory would be to see them, he thought, trying to imagine her reaction. After all these years to finally meet her brothers.

But why now? When he had so many things he needed to straighten out with her?

Please, Lord, help me to be happy for her. And for Joyce, he prayed.

"Before we go, I want to know if there's anything we need to know about Cory and Joyce," Jake said quietly. "Anything that might make a difference. For us."

Matthew pulled in one corner of his mouth as he thought. Should he tell them everything that had transpired the past few days? Should he get into the history of Zeke and the impact he had on their lives?

He decided to go for straightforward. It would take a long time and a lot of sharing before these two men would fully know what had happened in Joyce's and

Cory's lives. But they needed a couple of things now as he filled them in on Cory's background.

When he finished, Matthew leaned back against his desk, studying Jake and Simon, trying to imagine how Cory would react. In spite of his own mixed feelings he felt a stirring of anticipation and pleasure for Cory. "She has wanted to find you but hasn't had the resources or the time. Your mother has fibromyalgia. I'm not sure myself what it all means, but Cory has told me that it has given Joyce a lot of pain and has decreased her ability to work. The disease is often exacerbated by stress."

"How would our coming affect her?" Jake asked.

"To tell you the truth, I think a portion of her difficulty is directly connected to her feelings about giving you boys up. I am sure that finding out about you will make a huge difference for her."

Jake glanced at Simon again. Matthew could only guess as to what was going through their minds right now. Matthew's parents' marriage wasn't perfect, but all his life he had known the security of a stable family.

Jake and Simon had had to grow up with vague memories of another life, another mother. It must have been difficult.

Finally Simon stood. "I don't know about you, Jake, but I'm anxious to get this over and done with. This first meeting."

They shared a smile that Matthew was sure signified some common memory. Again he wondered how Cory would react to finally seeing the brothers she had been thinking of for so many years.

"Well, then, let's get going. You can follow me," Matthew offered, pushing away from his desk.

As they left the office, Matthew felt his heart pounding with a mixture of feelings he didn't know how to sort out. An eagerness to see Cory after being apart and a bittersweet pleasure for what he was about to witness.

"What is the matter with you, Cory?" Joyce asked as she came into the living room and saw Cory's flushed face.

"Matthew's coming," Cory called out just before she ducked into the bedroom. Running to her closet she riffled through the clothes. What should she wear?

Not enough time to think about that, she had to get her hair decent.

She ran across the hallway to the bathroom, pulled out her curling iron and plugged it in.

"Goodness, girl, what's gotten into you? I thought you weren't going to see him anymore."

Joyce stood in the doorway of the bathroom, frowning as Cory pulled out hairbrushes, some hair spray and her meager supply of makeup.

Cory looked up at her mother, fully aware of her disapproval. She stopped.

"I love him, Mother."

"Even after what he did?" Joyce's voice rang with disapproval.

"He didn't really do anything, now did he? It was Zeke who did everything." As she spoke, it was as if everything about her and Matthew's past and present realigned itself in her mind, in her life. "Even when they were defending him, it was Zeke who was chasing us, who was hounding you for visits. It was Zeke who did it all."

"They didn't have to help."

"If they didn't do it, someone else would have. And then who knows where we might have been?" Cory pulled the elastic out of her hair and began vigorously brushing her hair, anticipation and excitement making her awkward.

Joyce pursed her lips in reproach, crossing her arms tightly across her chest. "So now he's going to come here and sweep you off your feet, and you're going to leave."

Cory stopped what she was doing and then, as realization dawned, she lowered the brush. Setting it on the counter, she took her mother in her arms. "Mom, please don't think that. I haven't left you yet. I wouldn't leave you now."

Joyce held herself rigid, looking straight ahead.

Cory rubbed her mother's shoulders, her arms, as if trying to convince her with actions as well. "Mom, everything I've ever done has been for you. All the work, the decisions. Everything. Today, I want to think about me. Me and Matthew." It sounded selfish, but she knew that she had to be firm. "I love him. And I know he loves me."

"You can say that? After what he did?"

Cory shook her head. "I want to talk to him about that, but I think that what he did was because he was afraid." She was aware that she perfectly echoed Kelsey's words. "Not telling me about that second will didn't change anything."

"But he was the one who thought you should take it. Even though you didn't trust it."

"Matthew didn't know about Zeke. Didn't know what he was really like. He knows now."

"Just because you told him?" Joyce pulled back from her daughter, her expression pleading. "Please don't fall for the same thing I did, Cory. Don't let a man hurt you like Zeke hurt me. I know what love can do to a person. How it can blind you and make you unaware of anything else.''

Cory looked at her mother and in that moment realized the chance she was taking.

''Matthew told me he loves me, Mom.'' Cory smiled at the memory. ''And I guess, right now, I'm going to have to trust him. Because that's what love is all about. It's about taking chances.''

Joyce sniffed lightly. Blinking her eyes, she faced her daughter as if recognizing that she wasn't going to sway her. ''Then I guess you'll have to take them,'' she said as she turned and left the room.

Cory felt as if a support had been pulled away. It would have been so much easier to see Matthew again, knowing that her mother accepted her choice. A small niggling doubt wormed its way into her mind, but Cory dismissed it.

Please, Lord, I need Your blessing on this, she prayed, *I need to let go of my fears and doubts. I need to believe that Matthew loves me.* She looked at herself in the mirror and quickly brushed her hair. She was ready, she thought, and went to the living room. Twenty minutes later she was looking out the window. Surely Matthew should have been here by now? She went to the kitchen to make a cup of coffee.

The sharp peal of the doorbell made Cory jump.

''I'll get it,'' she called out, fairly flying down the hallway. She swung around the door frame into the living room and skidded to a halt just before the front entrance. Taking a calming breath, fingers fluttering over her hair, she stepped into the entrance and opened the front door.

Matthew stood framed in the opening, smiling a bemused smile. "Hi, there," he said quietly.

She felt as if she had to swallow to breathe. His voice, his face. So familiar to her. So dear. He had come.

"Hi, yourself," she said quietly, holding on to the edge of the door as if for support.

"I missed you." He lifted his hand, as if to touch her, then lowered it as he glanced behind him. Two strange men came up the walk and stopped on the stairs. Both tall. One with dark hair, dark eyes. He wore a denim jacket and blue jeans. The other had sandy-brown hair, hazel eyes. He wore a leather jacket over khaki pants. Not cops, that much she could tell.

"What's going on?" she whispered to Matthew, her heart beginning to pound with trepidation at the serious expressions on their faces. "What's wrong?"

"Nothing. Trust me, please." Matthew bit his lip, as their eyes met. He seemed to be pleading for understanding, as he drew her outside, his hand resting lightly on her shoulder.

"Cory, I'd like you to meet Jake and Simon Steele." Cory glanced back at him, puzzled, then back at the two men who hovered, waiting.

"They're your brothers," Matthew said, squeezing her shoulder gently.

Cory looked first at the dark-haired man, then the other one, trying to understand. Her breath left her chest as their names registered on her benumbed brain.

"Jake and Simon?" she whispered faintly, striving to understand, to accept. "My brothers?"

The lighter-haired one nodded. "We've been look-ing for you for a while," he said quietly. Then he took a step closer. "I'm Simon."

Cory glanced back at Matthew again, as if seeking approval.

"They're on the level, Cory." He lowered his hand, his fingers trailing down her arm.

Cory felt a wave of bewilderment flooding her senses as she looked back at them.

Yes, she could see in these tall, handsome men, traces of the younger brothers whose faces she knew by heart. In their faces she caught shifting glimpses of her mother and even herself.

The brothers she had prayed for and dreamed about. The brothers she had always thought would come swooping into her life to rescue her from Mat-thew, who now stood protectively behind her. Mat-thew whom she loved so desperately.

There was a dreamlike quality to the situation. No one moved as they took each other's measure.

"Cory, what's going on?"

Cory jumped as her mother spoke from the door-way behind Matthew.

Cory looked behind her as Joyce stepped past Mat-thew to stand beside her, then she looked back at the two men. "Jake and Simon are here," she said qui-etly, still unable to grasp the implications, the signif-icance of what was happening.

"Who...what...?" Joyce stammered.

"Jake and Simon. Your sons," Matthew said.

Joyce, too, glanced at Matthew, then back at the men. Her hands slowly crept upward to cover her mouth, as she repeated their names, then was utterly still.

It was as if they were frozen.

Cory and Joyce facing the men named Jake and Simon and behind them, Matthew.

Then Jake moved, taking Joyce's hands in his. "Mom," he said almost reverently.

Joyce reached up and, as she had done just moments ago with Cory, touched his face, tracing the lines, her expression bemused.

"Jake. My son."

Then she was enfolded gently in his arms as she started to cry.

Cory felt her throat thicken with emotion, still unable to completely absorb the reality of the scene. Her brothers. Here. They were real. Not some figment of her imagination.

Simon had taken her hand and was holding it, staring at her. "I have a sister," he said, shaking his head. "I have a beautiful little sister."

Then she, too, was pulled close in a rough embrace.

Simon pulled abruptly away, tapped Jake on the shoulder and then with a flurry of laughter and cries, Simon was hugging his mother and Jake held Cory.

Finally Joyce pulled away, her hands bracketing Simon's face as tears flowed freely down her own. "How did you find us? How did you know?"

Simon smiled down at her and gave her another quick hug. "Jake's lawyer found out," he said.

"My lawyer was contacted by Matthew asking if he knew a Jake and Simon who were brothers," Jake explained, his arm still holding Cory close. "After all these years, all it took was a few letters exchanged."

Cory then looked at Matthew who stood off to one side watching the tableau, smiling.

"You found them?" she asked, stepping away from Jake's embrace. "How did you do that?"

"A little luck and a few prayers," Matthew said, his smile bringing out the dimple that hovered beside his mouth.

Cory recognized the phrase from their first momentous meeting over a month ago, and she couldn't help but smile.

Then their eyes met, and their smiles faded away. Cory felt his gaze as tangibly as a touch. Her heart overflowed with love for him and without realizing it, she had taken a step closer to him.

"I think we better move inside," Simon said suddenly, breaking the moment between Matthew and Cory. "We've got lots to catch up on."

"Of course. Come in, come in." Joyce ushered them toward the door and Cory and Matthew trailed in their wake. Just before they stepped into the house, Cory felt Matthew's hand rest on her shoulder from behind as he bent his head closer.

"I need to talk to you, Cory," he pleaded, his breath warm against her neck.

She laid her hand on his and quickly glanced back, her heart going triple time as she took the plunge. "I love you," she said. She couldn't hold the words back any longer. In what was probably the most extraordinary moment of her life, she could not stop herself from expressing the emotion that filled her to overflowing.

Matthew's eyes darkened, his hand tightened on her shoulder. He moved closer.

Then Simon caught Cory's hand, pulling her into the house.

It would have to wait for later, Cory thought.

Chapter Sixteen

Inside the house was an air of celebration. Joyce fluttered back and forth, unable to take it all in.

"I'll make some coffee," Cory said quickly.

"I'll help you," Matthew volunteered.

As Cory tried to pour grounds into the coffee basket, her hands shook with an odd mixture of excitement at seeing her brothers and Matthew's nearness.

Matthew was laying out mugs on a tray, easily finding his way around the kitchen. They were both quiet, as if unable to find their way through this new predicament.

Cory finally got the coffeepot going, wiping her hands on a towel.

Then, Matthew came up behind her, slipped his arms around her and pulled her back against him. "I love you, Cory," he whispered against the side of her neck.

Cory let herself drift back against him, her hands clasping his arms. "I love you, too," she said softly, turning her head to look up at him.

He dropped a gentle kiss on her mouth, then gave her another one, slower this time.

Then he pulled away with a sigh of regret. "But your brothers are here now."

"I still can't believe it," she said, turning to face him. "And you did it."

Matthew smiled down at her, his fingers trailing up and down her arm. "With the Lord's help, Cory. Only with His help."

They shared the moment, then Cory stepped past him. "We better get this out there," she said quietly.

The next hour passed in a flurry of noise and laughter and memories. Cory found the photograph album and it was passed around. Simon had pictures of him and his wife, Caitlin. Jake, of his wife, Miriam, and daughter, Taryn.

"God has blessed us so richly," Simon was saying. "Caitlin is expecting. I can't believe the baby will have another aunt." Simon grinned at Cory and impulsively gave her another hug.

"What do you think Taryn will say, Jake?" Simon asked his brother.

"She'll be over the moon." Jake showed Cory a picture of his daughter standing in front of Miriam.

Cory took the picture, looking closely at Miriam. "She looks familiar," she said, trying to catch the memory.

"She's a model for a well-known cosmetics company," Jake said. "One more job and she's done. Thank goodness."

Cory shook her head in bewilderment. A sister-in-law who was a registered nurse, another who was a model. She couldn't help but wonder what they would think of someone who waited on tables for a living.

"When I told Miriam about you, she was so excited," Jake said. "She's never had a sister so she's pretty eager to meet you."

"I'm nothing special," Cory couldn't help but say.

Matthew caught her hand and when she looked at him, his expression was dead serious. "You're exceptional," he said, a thread of admonition in his voice.

"Miriam will give up that life without a second thought," Jake added quietly. "She would have traded all the fame in a heartbeat for the relationship you have with Mom."

Cory felt a surge of warmth toward her brother.

The talk started again, as stories were traded. Cory just listened, her hand still clasped in Matthew's. All through what her brothers said she felt their underlying pain as they yearned for the completeness of family. They all had their sorrows, she thought, but they also had their prayers and their faith and here they were together.

After a while, Jake said, "We know this is short notice, but we would love to have you come to the farm and spend some time with us. We have so much to catch up on."

"Of course. I'm not working. I would love to come." Joyce turned to Cory. "You can probably get time off, can't you?"

Cory nodded slowly. Once Kelsey got wind of what had just happened, she knew that her friend would move heaven and earth so that Cory could be with her brothers.

But did she want to go?

She glanced sidelong at Matthew. He got up, pulling Cory to her feet.

"If you'll excuse us a moment," he said to the group. Then without waiting for any acknowledgment, he led Cory outside.

On the front deck, away from everyone, he pulled her tightly into his arms.

"Oh, Cory, I wanted to do this the moment you opened the door," he said quietly. "But I couldn't. Not with your brothers breathing down my neck."

Cory returned his embrace, clinging to him, her heart overflowing with love and gratitude.

Once again they kissed, but this time with a fervor they couldn't express in front of everyone else.

"I need you, Cory. I missed you so much. I'm so sorry." His words rained down on her interspersed with kisses. "I wanted to tell you about the other will, but I was scared you would hate me."

"Never, Matthew. Never," she said, holding his face in her hands. "I'm sorry, too. I was wrong to be so angry with you, but it was such a disappointment."

"I know money isn't important to you, but I knew that you were making plans." Matthew sighed, toying with her hair, his fingers trailing down her neck. "I wanted to fix everything for you, make your life better. I want only good things for you, my dear."

"But you brought me my brothers." She smiled tremulously, tears threatening, her heart overflowing with happiness. "And you gave me the most beautiful doll in the world."

"You liked her?"

"I know what you were telling me, Matthew." She reached up and kissed him quickly again.

"So now your brothers want you to come for a visit." He sighed lightly in resignation. "You should go."

Cory nodded, realizing that he was right, yet she felt torn.

"I'd feel terrible if you didn't take this chance to get to know them, to spend some time at their place," he continued.

"I could do it later," she said slowly, considering the possibility.

"Maybe. But right now everything is so new, so exciting. Your mom would be so happy to have her whole family together for a while." Matthew dropped a light kiss on her forehead. "I told you I want only what is best for you. That's all."

"But to go now...."

"The timing isn't great. And if I had my way I'd keep you here, with me."

Cory smiled at that. "Okay. I'm glad that's settled."

"But I don't think it would be a good idea," he continued.

Cory's heart fell at that. "Why not?"

"Don't look at me like that, Cory. Let me explain it to you. I love you. You need to know that. But you also need to know that your needs are going to come first with me. I don't ever want you to think that I am anything remotely like Zeke Smith. I am not going to put what I want and what I think I need before your needs. And right now, I know you want to be with your brothers and your mother. As a family. You have never had that in your life. I know there might be other times and opportunities, but I feel that you should go with them. Not just for your mother's sake, not just for your brothers', but for your sake as well."

Cory felt the burden of the decision falling off her shoulder as Matthew spoke. And as she thought about what he said, she realized that he was right. She still felt torn between her love for Matthew and the fulfillment of her lifelong dream of reuniting her family, but she felt he was right.

"It won't be easy," she whispered. "I'll miss you."

"I'll miss you, too," he said, his expression serious. Then he kissed her quickly one more time, and led her back into the house.

Her brothers were overjoyed, her mother ecstatic and Cory was pleased that she had decided to go. Until she looked at Matthew.

Why did this all have to happen now? she thought ruefully. God's blessings were overwhelming her, and she didn't know which one to choose.

"No, you sit down. Simon and I will do the dishes."

Tilly, Jake's foster mother, gently eased Cory away from the sink. "You go sit in the living room and relax for a while. Or sit out on the porch. It's a lovely evening."

Cory opened her mouth to protest when Simon flicked a towel at her. "Let me try to make a good impression on Tilly," he said with a mock frown.

"I'll help, too," Caitlin offered.

"That's silly," Cory said. "You're expecting."

Caitlin rolled her eyes as she gathered up the cutlery from the table. "I'm hardly in a delicate condition. Just go and rest up. You'll need all the energy you can muster when we start playing Scrabble."

Cory frowned.

Caitlin grinned. "I know what you're thinking. Scrabble is hardly a contact sport, but once Simon starts playing a game, it's no holds barred. He plays to win and he cheats. It takes all our combined forces to keep an eye on him.''

"Hey," Simon protested, his hand over his heart. "I'm crushed."

Caitlin pointed a finger at him. "And you're toast." Caitlin grinned over her shoulder at Joyce and Cory. "We'll join you in a couple of minutes. I think you could probably use some time out from this character. I know I sure could."

With one more negated protest, Cory finally was convinced to leave. Fred, Jake's foster father, was dozing quietly in his recliner in the living room, so they walked quietly out onto the front porch.

The sun was heading down, its harsh afternoon rays softened by the encroaching evening. They sat together on the swing, Joyce letting out a contented sigh.

"It's so beautiful here, isn't it?"

Cory had to agree. It still felt strange to finally see her brother as a grown man. The shadowy figure that was forever young in her mind, was a farmer. That he had been raised by Fred and Tilly Prins who owned all this.

"It's been so busy the past couple of days, we haven't really had a chance to talk," Cory said, knowing that she had to bring up the subject that had been on her mind since this morning.

She missed Matthew. They had already been here a day and a half, and in good conscience she knew that she could go back.

It would just be hard to break it to her mother. Joyce who was a completely different woman since Jake and Simon had come into their lives.

Cory felt an easing of the burden as the brothers took over. As Miriam and Tilly and Caitlin all checked to see how Joyce was doing, made sure she was comfortable. Helped her with her exercises.

"It's overwhelming. All this family," Joyce said with a contented sigh. "My sons, back in my life again." She turned to Cory. "I'm so glad you came along," Joyce said, stroking her daughter's cheek. "So glad Matthew didn't convince you to stay."

"Matthew was the one who convinced me to go," Cory said.

Joyce frowned. "What? Then why…?"

"Why what?"

Joyce looked up, taking her daughter's hands in her own. "Just before you left, he asked me for permission to marry you. I thought he wanted you to stay with him."

Surprise trickled through Cory. Surprise and at the same time a conviction that she knew that this was the direction she and Matthew were headed.

"I thought it was too sudden," Joyce continued. "You've not been dating that long."

"But I've cared for him for longer than that," Cory admitted.

Joyce's hands squeezed Cory's. "I think I knew that, too," Joyce said quietly. "When you were younger I used to catch him looking at you. And once in a while, I caught you looking back. It made me nervous. Still does, a bit."

"Why? I love him. And I know that he loves me."

Joyce sighed, letting go of Cory's hands, staring off into the middle distance. Cory sensed her withdrawal into the past.

"What are you thinking of, Mom? That love can be blind, like you told me before Jake and Simon came? That I'm making a big mistake? Because I don't think I am, Mother.''

"I need to tell you something," Joyce said, her voice a thin sound. "I've wanted to tell you for some time now, but I couldn't. I just couldn't.'' She faltered, still looking away, rocking lightly now. "I wanted to tell you about Zeke. How guilty I felt about marrying him.''

"Mother, don't. It's over.''

"Maybe. But I need to tell you this.'' Joyce took in a slow breath, looking away from Cory, over the front lawn, surrounded by spruce trees. The secluded yard lent an air of intimacy to the front porch.

"I thought I was thinking of you when I said yes to Zeke. When he asked me to marry him. I thought I was giving you a father. But I wasn't. I was only thinking of myself and how much I loved him. Because I did. But I loved him even though I knew what he was like, Cory, even though I knew he didn't truly care for you. I thought he would change once we were married. I thought that he could grow to love you. I just didn't think it would turn out so badly." Joyce's voice faltered a moment. "I wish I could make it up to you, but I don't know how. I just don't know how.''

Cory could say nothing, feeling her mother's hurt, surprised at this new revelation.

"I've always had to live with that burden," Joyce continued, picking at a piece of lint on her sweater. "I've never been able to make it up to you, Cory. Lord knows I wanted to hundreds of times. Instead I ended up being a burden to you.''

Cory made a murmur of protest, but Joyce shook

her head. "It's true, Cory. It's been so difficult seeing you work so hard every day. Taking over for me when I couldn't do the one job I thought would help us out."

"Mother, you were never a burden," Cory blurted out.

"Yes, I was. You would have to be a saint not to feel some frustration when I had my really bad days and could barely get out of bed. I know you're no saint, but you came close, Cory." Her voice faltered, her hand caught Cory's in her own. "You came very close."

Cory didn't know what to say. She wanted to protest, but instead ended up agreeing. "It was hard and difficult," Cory replied. "But you know, Mom, everything that happened brought us to this place. Here. Now." As she spoke the words Cory realized the truth of what she was saying. "God used all the mistakes we made, and took all those tangled threads and brought us here. We found the boys because of Matthew. Matthew found us because of Zeke. And I found Matthew because of Zeke. And I love him."

Joyce smiled at her daughter, a smile of benediction. "I know you do. And in spite of the things I've said about him, I think you made a good choice."

Cory leaned over and carefully held her mother in her arms, unable to say anything. Joyce returned the hug, tears flowing quietly between them.

Joyce pulled away after a while, palming the moisture from her cheek. Her smile was tremulous. "I've always been so proud of you, Cory. Always." She drew in a deep breath and pulled her sweater closer around her. "Matthew has done things for you that Zeke never would have for me." She sighed lightly and faced her daughter again. "I know you miss him. And I know you feel torn. I'm so thankful that he convinced you to come. But you're right. You should go to him now."

"Thanks, Mom," she said softly. "Thanks for loving me."

"So I guess this is it for a while," Jake said, stopping his pickup in front of Matthew's office. "Do you want me to come in with you to make sure his intentions are honorable?"

Cory smiled at her big brother from the other side of the cab. It still seemed strange to think of this man she barely knew as the shadowy figures that had always been one of the brothers who would rescue her.

"No. He's already spoken to my mother, and she gave her blessing. Seems kind of old-fashioned, but I appreciate his doing it."

"From the way you talk about him, he seems like a decent man—" Jake shrugged "—for a lawyer."

"Don't start that," Cory warned.

"Do you know how many times Simon wanted to tell his lawyer jokes and Caitlin stopped him?" Jake said with a laugh.

"I probably know more than he does." Cory turned to Jake. "So I guess this is goodbye. For a while."

"It's been wonderful to see you, Cory. It was such an answer to prayer to connect with you, to spend time with you." He reached across the cab and caught her by the arm. "Come here so I can give you a brotherly hug."

Cory felt herself enveloped in arms clad in denim, pressed against a shirt smelling faintly of straw and that indefinable scent of outside. She hugged him tightly back, tears pricking the backs of her eyes.

"I'm so thankful," he said gruffly, pulling away to give her a quick kiss on her cheek. "God our Father is good," he said with a smile.

"Yes, He is," Cory said able to agree wholeheartedly with him on that.

"And now you want to go." Jake gave her another quick hug and then sat back. "Sure you don't want me to walk you to the door?"

Cory laughed as she slung her purse over her shoulder. "No. I'll be okay." She flashed him another quick grin, ran a hand over her hair and stepped out of the truck. She closed the door and waved at Jake, who merely waved back. He was going to wait until she was in the door, she realized.

And in that moment, she felt the security of family. Someone watching over her, concerned for her just because she was his sister.

She blew Jake a kiss and then with a grin she was unable to suppress, strode up the sidewalk to Matthew's office.

Another wave at the door and she was inside.

As the door fell slowly shut behind her, she felt an attack of nerves. Matthew was probably in the office.

Maybe. What if he was gone?

Other dreams had been snatched away from her at the last minute. Much of her life had been spent dealing with disappointment of one kind or another.

But she had just seen the brothers she never thought she would. Just before she left Matthew had told her he loved her.

Please, Lord, I've been through enough in my life, she prayed. *Let me cling to the promise that Matthew gave me. Help me to trust that he loves me. Help me to trust him.*

She drew in a deep breath, sent up one more quick prayer and stepped through the doors into the main area of the office.

The secretary looked up at her, then smiled. "Matthew is in his office," she said. "Shall I tell him you're here?"

"No, that's okay," Cory said running a nervous hand over her hair. "I'll just go in."

She took another deep breath, walked resolutely over to his door and slowly opened it.

Matthew was standing with his back to the room, staring out the window of his office. He hadn't heard the door open. Cory stepped quietly inside, closing the door behind her, content for now just to watch him.

He reached up and plowed his fingers through his hair, rearranging the neat waves. Then he sighed. He wasn't wearing his suit jacket, and wrinkles crisscrossed his shirt. He didn't look like the put-together young lawyer he usually did.

Then she saw it. On the desk was a picture of her at her prom. She and Deirdre were standing together, laughing at the camera.

But even more touching was what was in front of the picture. A small velvet box.

Because of what Matthew had asked her mother, she was pretty sure she knew what was in it.

Cory felt a rush of love for him, felt her heart begin to quicken in anticipation.

Then, as if he sensed her presence, he turned around. He looked bemused, then puzzled.

"Cory?" he asked, frowning. Then, recognition

dawned and he was across the room in a couple of steps, hauling her against him.

"Oh, Cory. I missed you, I missed you."

And as she clung to him, returning his embrace, all her niggling doubts and worries melted away.

"I missed you, too," she said, her voice muffled against his shirt.

He drew back just enough to kiss her soundly, to frame her face with his hands as his eyes traveled over her every feature.

"You're back already," he said, wonderment tingeing his voice.

"I couldn't stay any longer," she confessed. Then, just because she could, she reached up, messed his hair and then rearranged it. "I love you," she said simply.

Matthew sighed and gently drew her close again, his face buried in her hair. "That sounds so good to me."

"I love you," she repeated.

He drew back again, shaking his head. "I can't believe you're here."

"I can. I made Jake drive faster than he wanted so that I could get here in four hours, instead of five."

"And why did you want to do that?" he asked, a teasing note in his voice.

"So that you could propose to me?" she said, confidence giving her a boldness she didn't think she possessed.

"You guessed."

"No. My mother told me you asked her. And I saw the jeweler's box on your desk."

Matthew twisted around, glancing over his shoulder. "Oh. That box." He released her and picked it up. He carefully opened it and took the ring out, making a pretense of looking at it carefully.

"Did you know that marriage is the only adventure available to all men?" he said with a slow grin.

Cory looked at the ring, then back at him. She couldn't think of anything to say.

"So, Cory Luciuk. Will you marry me?"

To her surprise and slight chagrin she felt tears pool in her eyes. She blinked, then blinked again, but she couldn't stop their gentle coursing down her cheek.

"Yes, I will," she said softly, as Matthew slipped the ring on her finger.

Matthew held her close. Kissed her once more. "I feel I should tell you...I'm still working on Zeke's will."

Cory laid her finger on his mouth. "I told you I didn't want anything from Zeke." She traced the line of his mouth, felt the faint rasp of stubble on his cheek. "My mother doesn't either. Let that woman have it." Cory leaned back in his arms, clasping her hands behind his neck. "I have everything I want. Right now. Right here."

And as they embraced once more, she sent up a prayer of thanks that not all the prayers in her life had been answered.

Epilogue

"Hold still, Cory," Kelsey admonished. She fluffed out the back of Cory's wedding dress, adjusted the train and then stepped back. "There. Now it's perfect."

"It was fine before," Cory muttered, pressing her hand against her stomach. As if that would ease the butterflies in it.

"I can't believe how nice you clean up," Kelsey said, walking around, adjusting here, tugging there. "Such a gorgeous dress."

The silk shimmered under the bright light of the church foyer. The narrow band of beading decorating the off-the-shoulder band was echoed at the Elizabethan style waist and along the bottom of the dress.

"Are we ready?" Simon asked, fidgeting on one side of his sister. Cory gave him a quick, sidelong glance, hardly daring to move lest Kelsey start fussing again. He looked tamed down in his suit, his hair smoothed down. Jake stood on her right, staring straight ahead, his expression solemn. Cory felt a burst of pride at her handsome brothers, so thankful that they could be the ones to bring her down the aisle.

"I think we're ready," Kelsey said. She gave her own rust-coloured dress a quick once-over, adjusted Jake's daughter Taryn's headpiece and handed Chris the pillow with the rings on it.

"Looking good everyone," she said, giving Cory's brothers an appreciative look.

She tweaked one of the lilies in Cory's bouquet, gave her a quick kiss for luck and then turned to signal the organist.

The organ struck up the wedding march and with one last giggling glance over her shoulder, Taryn stepped out into the aisle, the flowers woven through her head bobbing with every step she took. She clung to Chris's hand with a death grip, but Chris didn't seem to mind.

Kelsey gave her friend one more grin then stepped out herself.

Cory took a slow, deep breath, glancing first to her right, then to her left.

Jake smiled a brotherly smile, Simon winked at her.

"Shall we go?" Jake asked, holding out his arm.

"I'm ready," Cory said. She tucked her right arm through his, transferred her bouquet to that hand and then, with a cheeky grin at Simon slipped her arm through his as well.

"Do you think we'll all fit in the aisle?" Simon whispered, rearranging her veil so that it lay gossamer fine over her shoulders.

"Can we do this?" Jake said sternly, ever the older brother.

Simon winked at Cory once again and as quickly, rearranged his features into a solemn expression.

Cory suppressed a giggle and on Jake's count, they began the long, slow journey.

Lightbulbs flashed, faces smiled back, she heard faint expressions of appreciation as they made their way down the aisle, the joyful strains of the organ filling the church.

Then, past the craning necks, just beyond the crowd of people, she saw Matthew. He stood in the front of the church, his hands clasped in front of him in typical nervous groom fashion.

His hair had been tamed but still curled at the ends. His dark suit set off his startling white shirt, which in turn set off the bright green of his eyes.

Their eyes met and for a moment Cory almost had to laugh at the irony of the whole situation.

As she walked down the aisle, flanked by her brothers Cory realized that at one time in her life she had actively prayed for these same men to come swooping into her life to rescue her from the man they were now walking toward. The man she was about to pledge her life, her loyalty and love.

Again she sent up a prayer of thanks that God worked His own way in her life.

They made it to the front, Kelsey smiling, Taryn still giggling.

As the minister asked who gave this woman, Jake and Simon glanced at Joyce who slowly stood up.

"We all do," Jake said firmly.

Then with a gentle kiss from each of her brothers she was handed over to Matthew.

Imperceptibly he shook his head in wonder, his expression enthralled.

"You're beautiful," he whispered, as he took her arm.

The ceremony went by as if in a dream. All Cory could remember was the reassuring pressure of Matthew's cool hands, his gentle smile and the sincerity in his voice as, before God and His people, he pledged his love and loyalty to Cory Luciuk.

The minister pronounced the blessing, introduced them as husband and wife. Before them Cory saw the smiling faces of her brothers and their wives. Her mother was crying, as was Matthew's, but Cory knew they were tears of happiness. Clifton smiled at both of them, as if in benediction.

Then, with a burst of triumphant music from the organ ringing in their ears and the blessing of beaming faces surrounding them, Cory and Matthew strode down the aisle.

Mr. and Mrs. McKnight.

More hugs and more felicitations as fellow church members and friends gathered to congratulate them.

Cory felt as if her face was going to crack from smiling so much, but she couldn't stop. Through all the noise and congratulations, she was constantly aware of Matthew at her side. Whenever he had a chance, he would give her a quick, one-armed hug, pulling her close to him.

To Cory's surprise even Deirdre had shown up, looking satisfied with her cousin and her old friend.

At last the lineup was done.

"I need a group picture at the front of the church," the photographer called out. "Just the family for now please."

Cory and Matthew walked back to the front of the

church, and stood where the photographer directed them.

"Okay, other family members."

They were immediately surrounded. Clifton and Nancy on one side, Joyce on the other. Jake, Miriam, Taryn. Simon and Caitlin filled in the gaps.

As they jostled each other, following the photographer's directions, Matthew gave Cory another hug. "I didn't know I was getting such a rowdy family," he said, grinning down into her smiling face.

From the security of her husband's arms, Cory looked around.

"We're a family," she breathed in wonder, as she carefully blinked back a sudden rush of tears. Jake caught her eye, smiling back at her. She turned to Simon who had a self-satisfied grin plastered on his face. He gave her a quick thumbs-up.

Joyce beamed back at her daughter.

Lastly Cory looked back at her beloved husband who had a part in bringing them all together.

"We're a family at last," she said, her voice filled with wonder.

Matthew dropped a light kiss on her forehead. "And God willing, we're going to make our own family," he said, adjusting her veil.

She gazed at him, with all the love in her heart shining in her eyes.

"Okay, family, smile at the camera," ordered the photographer.

And the family did.

* * * * *

Dear Reader,

This is the last book in the STEALING HOME
series, and I wrote it with mixed feelings. I could
finally bring this family together, but by doing that,
it meant saying goodbye to the characters. I know they
are only characters, but for the past year and a half they
were a part of my life. I know there are families out
there who hurt and hunger, and I pray for them that
through God, they might find peace and each other.
I also pray for those who do not have the support of
family. May you, too, trust that God can be mother and
father, sister and brother to you.

Carolyne Aarsen